1: SAVING PAUL

"I must save him, Mary. I must!" Jane insisted, as she had so many times before, causing Mary Pappas, her dear friend and dressmaker, to groan inwardly and roll her eyes outwardly.

Mary had heard Jane's complaint at least once every hour—and there had been many—that the women had spent together for the last two months since Paul's letter arrived. He had written of his intention to stay in Greece and surrender his American citizenship by joining the Greek army. Her advice on the problem had gone unheeded, but she loved the family—Jane especially, but John, her husband, and Paul, her son, as well—and so she had begun again to reason with her friend.

"He's a grown man now, Jane, and he must make his own life decisions."

"Physically, yes, but he's still a baby in everything else."

"He's doing postgraduate study at the University of Athens; give him credit for a good mind."

"He has problems there."

"His mind?"

"He had an accident."

"What happened?"

Now it was Jane's turn to roll her eyes. Paul's problem was a subject she didn't discuss with anyone, not even with John, at least not after Paul had recovered from the immediate danger of his injury. But now she had a great need to expiate her thoughts and feelings.

I was at fault.

Was I at fault?

How could my attention have wandered?

Little Paul had had time to open the door and fall out of the moving car. He'd only been a child, six years old and precocious to a fault.

I am his mother.
I was responsible.
Wasn't I?

She had been seated in the front passenger seat, and he had been in the back, directly behind her.

What had she and John been arguing about? As if she could ever forget! About Paul's hair! It was so lovely, long and curly, midnight black, and shiny. John had been asking her to get it cut, but she couldn't bear the idea. However, she was reasonable; she did trim the unruly swatches, but only by her loving hand, and she saved the shorn locks.

"Ioanna!"

He had called her Ioanna only once before, when he'd proposed marriage. But the second use alerted her and caused her to stiffen. She knew what was coming. She wouldn't give in; her boy would keep his beautiful mane for at least another year.

"Ioanna," John began again now that he had her attention, and in the tone of his voice, there was no ambiguity, "if you do not take him barber, I will!

"I ask you, and nice, and many times, and now I order you get him haircut. He looks like girl. My son looks like female!"

If only John hadn't used that word: "order." I order you! If he had said, "Now I plead with you again," she might have reconsidered.

But ordered? Never!

She was the mother. She had gone through the pregnancy, carried the embryo, created Paul. A remarkable experience; she'd known the moment she'd conceived, had felt it, and she had so enjoyed the feeling of the life growing within her that she'd wanted to hold the child back from the world just a little longer. They had a closeness beyond the obvious physical, a bond of understanding between them. Three hundred and one days, three of the most glorious weeks "late." A typical man, the doctor had warned that the delivery should be by cesarean section and soon, no, immediately, as the baby had grown too large to safely exit by the birth canal. When she'd recovered from the surgery, they had loaded her arms with her twenty-six-inch-long, twelve-pound-ten-ounce frowning

CONTENTS:

baby boy who looked ready to conquer the world, and her dreams of his success had been cemented when the obstetrician had said, "Put books under his arms and send him to school."

He didn't look like a girl. He was cute, adorably.

"You order me, Ioannis?" Jane had asked incredulously. Since he had called her Ioanna, she'd hit right back with the Greek version of his name. And Ioannis and Ioanna, or John and Jane, were off, launched on the beginning of an argument that would become—to an impartial observer—the salient feature of their marriage, and parenting as well.

* * *

True, John had bought her a new car, a 1946 Nash 600, but she had wanted a Buick Super 8, not a Nash.

However, John had insisted on the Nash because he could use it as a delivery vehicle in an emergency.

The Nash was a four-door model that had retained the "suicide doors," or hinged-at-the-rear design for the back doors from the era of horse-drawn carriages, and John's clever foreman at the pie factory would make the center post between the front and rear doors removable, allowing large bread trays and pie pans to be stacked within the car cabin when the passenger and rear seats were removed. The model's large baggage trunk provided additional space.

She had not been pleased with the new car, but she was desperately happy to get rid of the old one, a 1937 Plymouth coupe that had an ugly, frog-like design and steered as she imagined a battle tank would.

But suicide-style doors on a family car was not a good idea, even when partially redeemed by the clever linkage of the front door lock and the lock on the rear door of the same side so that the unlocking of the rear was impossible as long as the front button was depressed. Still, Jane preferred the Buick, which did not rely on a fancy locking mechanism, because it did not have suicide-style doors.

Jane and John had decided to pick Paul up from school on the day they took delivery of their Nash. Paul had helped his father select it from the manufacturer's catalogs, and Paul knew all of its latest refinements even better than John did.

Paul was so bright, Jane remembered; he had such a vivid imagination and yet remained ever aware of the present. He thrilled her when he so forcibly described his magical world to her Russian friend, Titania, who was also an exiled Russian countess, that she petted the kitten he told her was curled on her lap.

Cats! He loved cats. He filled every room with them, especially wherever she was working. He squealed and immediately pleaded with her to be more careful when walking to avoid stepping on any of the foolish kittens. She counseled him to gather his pride and explain to them that they must scurry away from her footsteps, as she was busy keeping them all happy and fed and often couldn't change her course to avoid a stray tail.

And he had. And she had felt warm and smiled when she'd overheard him instructing his feline friends, "All of you, even the little ones, must stay out of Mommy's way."

They arrived as Paul was exiting the playground of the school; he was holding hands with his first-grade crush, Susie, and they were preparing to walk home together on Susie's side of the road, not Paul's, as she lived across the street and a block farther than he did.

On picking up Paul, who was very excited about the arrival of the new Nash, John and Jane agreed to give Susie a ride home, even if that meant Paul would be sitting in the back seat with Susie instead of up front between them, and attention was given by both parents to insuring that the buttons for the front door locks on both sides of the new car were in the locked position, meaning the two children in the backseat were in a protected space. Of course, Jane had paid attention to their play, happy again as Paul was explaining to Susie all the wonders of this model Nash, like the concealed fold-down armrests, and an ashtray wonderfully integrated with the drive-train tunnel, and the little, rounded corner, triangular side windows that unlatched when you pressed a little knob on the handle and then turned it up, and the removable floor mats, and the crank that lowered and raised the main window, and the door handle that was pulled up to open but wouldn't move when the front door button was depressed.

"I'll show you, Su-si-e—"

Jane felt the blast of cold air and heard Susie's scream and turned in time to see Paul still flying through the air as the rushing wind of the car's velocity blasted open the suicide door and flung him out of the car.

"John!" she screamed.

He had already slammed on the brakes.

The damage had been done; Paul had slid on the roadside ice, stopping abruptly when his head had banged against the curb.

In the emergency room, they shaved Paul's hair to the scalp. When Jane learned later that the medical cleanup crew had swept his shed locks into the trash, she fainted.

Paul's skull was compound fractured with two long, narrow, dented breaks, and the concussion was severe, possibly causing irreversible mental impairment.

* * *

Jane's enjoyment of mothering ended as the accident replaced her smart, active, social son with a dull-witted, uncoordinated, introverted child. Her despair was magnified when she learned that Paul remembered himself as he had been before the accident and asked her where his other parts had gone because he no longer had them. In their place, he complained of a lead cap that pressed against his brain and was so heavy it made him stoop.

"He isn't right, Mary; he never was after the accident."

"But you make him sound like a brick, and he's not."

"No, he worked hard to overcome his deficits, and we sent him to the best schools."

"You mean not locally, because I don't think any of the schools here are good."

"Well, we couldn't send him away too young. Maybe, though, we should have put him in a boarding school much earlier if we had found a good school directed toward remedial students. It was just so hard to know what to do. After the war, everything turned bad... I mean, John was on the verge of collapse from exhaustion because he was running the bakery by himself, and Paul had suffered the concussion, but as if that wasn't enough in itself, before his enforced period of immobility ended, he caught chicken pox in the hospital. They were going to put him in quarantine, but I persuaded the doctor to let me take him home instead, and the doctor agreed, more because he was impressed by the way Paul had kept his promise and did not move his head. But fevers and inactivity led to Bright's disease.

"Mary," Jane said, looking tragic, "for months, it seemed that as Paul got over one thing, something else knocked him down, and I was fearful for his life. And even if he recovered from everything else, there was still the threat that his mind would be forever clouded by the concussion. And really, Arkansas's inferior school system was part of the reason we decided to buy the DeSoto and move here. He'd been so bright that his first-grade teacher in Illinois thought he could catch up even though he'd missed two thirds of the school year. But in the meantime, we moved closer to John's pie company, and that meant Paul would begin the second grade in an urban school instead of the suburban one where he'd started. In the city, they were less sympathetic to his condition. At the end of the second month—well, before Thanksgiving—the school counselor called us in and warned us that he would not pass Paul on to third grade, nor would he hold him in the second another year but, in fact, would recommend that he do the first over again."

"How much of this does Paul know?"

"Why, all of it, of course.

"No, that's wrong. He doesn't know that if we had stayed in Illinois, he would have gone back to the first grade instead of on to the third. But after the accident, he had so little confidence in anything he did that I thought setting him back two school years would just have crushed him with more problems.

"And no, I don't think he realizes how close he came to ending up in a vegetative state."

"That bad!"

"He says that he remembers the doctor giving him the choice to either hold and keep his head absolutely still from his own volition for twenty-one days or have it encircled with sand-bags and held down with head braces that would not allow him to move it. And how the doctor asked him, after he promised not to move by himself, if he realized how long twenty-one days was. And Paul answered, 'Almost till Christmas,'" Jane sobbed. "He knew it was the second of December because the school holiday would start in two weeks and he was so looking forward to it."

"You see," Mary interjected, "the accident couldn't have retarded him severely if he could still think that out."

"That was at the beginning, but afterwards, he just got duller by the day."

The two women remained silent.

Mary dipped her head, nodding down and to the left, and compressed the parting of her lips into a line. She continued her sewing. She couldn't picture Paul as mentally defective; granted, he was disorganized to a fault and very aggressive, especially toward Jane, and not much less with John. With other people, he was reasonable if he knew them well, shy if not, but not with his parents. They—in her estimation—interfered with him far more than they should have. Their excuse, she allowed, must have arisen from over protectiveness inspired in them after the accident. And from things Paul had told her, she understood that part of his aggressiveness was a reaction to it, to their attempt to manage every aspect of his life.

Paul was in Greece; there was nothing she could do for him, but Jane was sitting on the couch opposite her in the small living room of her suite in the Virginia Apartments across Canyon Street from the DeSoto Hotel & Baths.

Mary was twenty years Jane's senior, but after the age of fifty, people were all just old.

She was.

She felt her years and her pain.

The pain was always there in her legs, especially the right one. The thermal baths helped, but the broken and fractured bones had been operated on and pinned so many times that nothing but a new beginning would suffice to relieve the endless ache.

Her life had been a continuous travail, but it could have been worse: she might not have lived at all. Her twin sister, Anna, had died a week after birth, and her younger brother, Alexandros—but they had called him Alekos—had passed when he was ten, and shortly thereafter, both her parents had been killed when the 7.4 Richter scale earthquake tumbled their house upon them and devastated Zakynthos, her native island, in 1905.

At fourteen, Mary had claimed sixteen, and she'd had the figure to support it; she applied to the marriage bureau to become a mail-order bride of one of the island's native sons who had immigrated to America. She was beautiful, as young girls often are, and fit, and her desirable condition and qualities were evident even in grainy photographs. A match was quickly arranged, and Mary arrived in New York on the 1st of January, 1906, to become the wife of Peter Pappas. He met the boat—brides were often misappropriated, as interlopers abounded—and carried his fiancée via the 20th Century Limited express train to Joliet, Illinois, where he lived. Married quickly, with the bride in white, at the local Greek Orthodox church for propriety's sake, the new man and wife were anything but compatible; unfortunately, they had exchanged vows before learning their dissimilarities. Still, had they known of the melee in waiting, would it have changed anything? Necessity imposes its own set of rules.

Of the outer differences, Peter was large, both tall and portly, while Mary was petite. He was aggressive and outgoing; she was shy and retiring. He, crude and a man of action; she was delicate and contemplative—even at fourteen.

Averaging one per year, Mary suffered a series of miscarriages, the last of which was a premature cesarean still-birth; a hysterectomy was indicated and performed, as Mary could probably not survive another pregnancy, nor was the embryo likely to be viable.

Thus, since Peter could not produce progeny with her, he sought and found other sources.

Fortunately, the couple had purchased a small hotel with fourteen rooms in downtown Joliet, and to this enterprise, Mary had devoted her time and energy; she rarely saw Peter either for work or bed or companionship. And then, one morning in the tenth year of their marriage—or whatever it was they shared—she awoke to the news that Peter, or what was left of him, had been struck on his vehicle's driver-side door by a fast-moving freight train at an unguarded crossing on his way back from a South Side Chicago loose-female-and-hard-liquor-studded party.

Peter's will bequeathed Mary one dollar and the hotel; his cash and other valuables were designated for various personages with spicier names like Candice and Juliette.

She was forced to dismiss all her hotel staff except one maid and a young do-it-all handyman. The roof of the four-story building, which was topped with an elevator motor room, was always leaking somewhere, window sashes were always sticking, and the elevator itself was in need of constant maintenance.

One day, Mary ascended by the laboring, lumbering contraption and darted out onto the third floor to do an errand and then return a basket of soiled linens to the ground floor.

Their rule was to close the mesh-style sliding metal fence that served as the elevator's door when the carriage was on another floor, but when it was on the same floor, they often left the gate open, especially when they would be entering the contraption with their arms full.

The handyman was in the motor room on the roof, and he was testing the copper strip switches that were activated by pull cords that hung at a convenient height beside the shaft on each floor; if the left cord was pulled, the elevator descended, but with a pull of the right, it ascended.

Mary, her mind busy turning the mild grief she felt for the recent loss of Peter into a determination to make a success of the hotel, her arms holding a large laundry basket in front of her, having just moments before used the elevator and left the sliding cage door open, walked into space three stories above the basement.

The handyman's adjustments had elevated the carriage to the fourth floor; he had not known Mary's whereabouts or what she was doing.

The laundry basket, an open-weave wicker construction, full of sheets, towels, blankets, and even a pillow or two, saved her life, but her legs were smashed, especially the right one that fell upon and was mangled by one of the spring mechanisms that was meant to cushion the carriage if the lifting cable snapped and it dropped. Fortunately, she was able to scream before she passed out; the maid discovered her and called for help as well as to the handyman not to bring the elevator down.

She survived, endured numerous operations, and, by the combined effect of her will and the thermal baths of Hot Springs National Park, Arkansas, of which she took a three-week course every six months, walked with only a cane.

But now she was a permanent resident of Hot Springs, having sold the hotel and taken her pension, and she was taking a thermal bath every day, as she would soon leave for Greece to return to Zakynthos and build an earthquake-proof one-story home on an old orchard that she had inherited near her native village. She was hoping that the healing powers of the radon-gas-containing mineral waters could be banked, because she would not return—too old— to the U.S. She would be sailing from New Orleans to Piraeus, and she had suggested that Jane come with her, especially since Jane was so worried about Paul.

"Let us—purely for the sake of argument—say that your suspicion is right, that Paul has gotten mixed up with a woman," Mary began.

"He said she is English but knows Greek well, and that her name is Judy," Jane supplied.

"And they are staying together—I mean, Paul with this Judy?"

"He says they share the rent, but I fear it's much more than that."

"He's a young man, Jane; wouldn't he have relations with a woman?"

"That's bad enough!

"Even if she speaks Greek, she's not Greek. And she must be filling Paul's mind with all kinds of ideas. How could he even consider giving up his American citizenship? Everyone in the world wants to become one, and he's native born but is considering giving it up?

"Don't you see? He's not thinking, and it's my fault. If I had been paying more attention, I could have saved him from the accident then, and there wouldn't be this problem now."

"You think the accident changed his character?"

"Of course it did; all his cousins are normal people. I'm normal. John's normal. There's no history of insanity in his or my family line."

"You go too far. He's not insane."

"I don't mean clinically insane. I just mean he's not normal. He isn't thinking correctly, because he can't. All the opportunities are here, not in Greece. Can't he see that?"

"He's young; he wants adventure."

"And I was afraid of that. I didn't want to let him go, but I couldn't stop him. He was over twenty-one. He got his own passport when he turned eighteen—we had a family one before. We wouldn't give him any money, but he didn't want any. While he was a student at Northwestern, he worked at a bookstore, and during the last six months before graduation, he didn't buy any books, because, before then, his pay never equaled his purchases. He had saved enough to buy a one-way plane ticket, and he had five hundred dollars in cash. But he had anticipated us on another matter. John and the president of the local draft board were good friends from the Lions Club. John decided to ask McCain to draft Paul immediately after the summer following his graduation. We wanted to take a vacation before Paul went in, because he wouldn't be available to relieve us for at least two years. But Paul had applied for a year's deferment from military service for postgraduate studies overseas, and it had been approved before John spoke to McCain. They couldn't take it back because it had gone through channels and would have needed a sufficient reason that they did not have since Paul hadn't done anything to invalidate the deferment except displease his parents. John did get McCain to promise that the service deferment would not be extended for any reason, even valid ones."

"That was not fair," Mary objected, beginning to realize that she needed to protect Paul rather than abet Jane.

"Fair!" Jane exclaimed. "What's fair about Paul's threat?"

"But did he state it as a threat or just as his plan, letting you know what he intended to do?"

"Mary, I can't believe you would support Paul."

"I'm not, Jane. I am just trying to be objective. If you don't look at this situation calmly, you are going to make big mistakes, I fear."

"I tell you his future is here with us in the business, and there are some perfectly lovely young Greek girls for him to marry after he does his military service.

"But there! That's another sign that he is not right in his head. John could get him out of having to go at all. McCain told him. You don't see any other young men from our class going into the army unless they're making it a profession. John told Paul he could get out, but Paul, although he hates discipline, refused the offer! You see! He's not thinking straight about anything. He's been caught by a gold-digging, predatory, unclean foreign female; he could get out of military service completely, but he plans to join the Greek army, and it must be much worse than the American. Don't you see? He would give up American citizenship to live in Greece the rest of his life like a pauper.

"Need I tell you more?" was Jane's sad rhetorical question.

2: DUMB BUNNY

Paul, on the other hand, frantic Jane's half-idiot but beloved son, was having a ball. He couldn't get enough of everything: clear, warm blue skies; coarse blond sand shorelines; seas turning midnight bluer with depth; young, sexual, naked women on beaches; olive oil and oregano of the highest quality and in copious quantities; studying at the university in the rich language that he so desperately wanted to learn well; aromatic, warm bread loafs bought fresh for two pennies from the bakery at every meal; being amongst people who lived for joy even when conditions were horrible; places to go, experiences to have, things to learn—learn—learn—and there was no end to the new and unknown; islands to visit; sensible mountains to climb; walking, walking everywhere in the city and even many places in the countryside; living in Anafiotika, at the heart of the Plaka, in the center of Athens, on the slopes of the Acropolis; pretending to be real.

* * *

He had been writing long letters to his cousin Jimmy who was living in Hot Springs and working at the De Soto as a diary, sending them, of course, not holding them back, knowing Jimmy would never show the originals to his parents but would extrapolate the message Paul wanted to convey to them by revealing his progressively more emphatic declarations that he was not a Greek-American but rather a Greek who'd been born in the U.S.

> Dear Jimmy,
> I know that a place is not a living organism, at least not in our ordinary way of thinking, and thus, it cannot represent, or express, human or even lifelike characteristics. However, I de-

clare that Anafiotika is my friend. Syntax allows my claim by classifying it as "poetic fallacy." Okay, so allow me to describe my life as if everything around is alive and I am an organic unit in a sea of others, some of which we all recognize the forms thereof and others that only fallible poets see.

I begin my tales, then, in perceptual error, and I admit that I am likely to end them in the same vein, that is, in suspended stride, as things that do not end when they stop.

Greece, as nowhere else I've been, is alive. The land lives. Not just the sun, but Helios, shines. The spirits of history are at my shoulders, around my body, filling my mind. Can we accept that our immediate, greater living creature—no, relative—is the Earth, the planet itself, and then imagine that in certain places, the life processes of our ocean-washed rocky home issue from the surroundings to awaken even a dumb bunny like me? I see the best we—no, strike we—the best that I can do is try to live with the Earth as a symbiont, but the worst of my efforts—and that of others—is to become parasitic. Here, people are more of the first nature; in the U.S., in my opinion, the second nature prevails.

But I fear that a large part of the greater awareness of the Greeks is due to poverty. When you're poor, you are obliged to notice what is happening around you, and it is easier to see that people can survive cooperatively or exhaust themselves competitively.

We travel a lot, hitchhiking around the county, and in so many places, I am overcome with awe, that wonderful feeling of being so small. And at the end of the journey, we return to Anafiotika, which will be here after we have turned to dust, and has been here and will continue to be here as we come and go for our brief period of time among the little houses and alleys in the warm heart of Plaka in the small but diverse neighborhood where the ratio is about one foreign resident for every six locals, or, like me, half-assed Greeks who have the blood but not the experiences.

Our foreign enclave consists of twelve friends making five couples, one of whom is homosexual, plus a free-agent young woman, and a promiscuous Irishman. We also include transients who come and stay for weeks or months; they are few but colorful.

I didn't mention this in my first letters because its prophetic nature was not apparent to me then, but back to my initial arrival. I had a brief encounter with an older man who was deplaning ahead of me. When he got to the bottom of the staircase platform and had set both feet on the tarmac, he moved to the side, out of the way of those of us behind, and he knelt down on his knees and then bent forward and kissed the ground and touched his forehead to it. When I descended beside him, I did the same. He looked at me and said, "I was your age when I left." Then he pointed to the asphalt and added, "Tar is not soil, but when I get home to my island, to my village, I will kiss the earth, the soil, the rocks, the sunbeams, the very dust if I can."

So, I answered, "You're lucky. You don't have to leave."

"You do?"

"Yeah, I've only got a year."

"Ah," he said, and his eyes sparkled like yours do when you're up to something sneaky, "but in Greece, you can pack a lifetime into a year."

It was like he foretold my future, or ordained it. I suddenly felt as I rose again to my feet and continued walking toward passport control that his words had swept my mind clean and opened it to countless new experiences.

Anyway, I took the bus to Piraeus and, from the terminus, walked to your old place; nothing had changed along the way in the two years of my absence. Aliki was at home; you had written her to expect me.

If anything, Jimmy, she's uglier than ever. Really depressed over your leaving. And on top of all her ghastly physical characteristics, loneliness now weighs down on every aspect of her person. Her heart, of course, is as always, pure generosity, and she sends you many thanks for the money you give her each month and the extra fifty you entrusted to me for her.

She had prepared wild greens and *skordiala* and a wonderfully baked red snapper for our lunch. Delicious, as you well know.

It's so strange, isn't it? You look at Aliki's youthful photographs when she was very pretty, if not absolutely beautiful, and then turn back to the present and see the hag she has become. My god, I fear there's a lesson in what's happened to her that I don't want to learn, or even think about.

Aliki wasn't at all happy that I intended to leave on the next boat for Mykonos. She wanted to hear all about you and how you were and did I think you would ever come back and on and on—all of it about you, and each subject inexhaustible.

Anyway, Aliki had made the bed in your old room for me, and I swear that it is exactly as you had left it—at least, as I saw it last—two years ago.

In spite of her desire that I stay at least a few days more, she supplied me with bacon sandwiches for the boat trip, and I left for Mykonos the following afternoon. On the stern open deck, I saw this woman who turned out to be Judy. She was speaking French to a vagabond-type guy, and I was talking in Greek to a Tinian lad. Our conversations ended almost simultaneously, and we were alone.

"I heard a distinct American accent to your Greek. Are you?" she asked.

"What can I say?" I answered, and then I asked, "And what are you?"

"British."

"That's great," I said, and we continued in English. You know the stuff, we each told the other our condensed life stories, and then we played chess—she had a portable set—and we drank a couple of *ouzos*, smoked one cigarette after another, and flirted openly on both sides. "Bravo, Paul," I said to myself. "Second day in Greece, and you've already scored a chick." But there had been that one little exception on her part, that omission in her story that shot me down when we disembarked on Mykonos.

Consolation prize: Judy wasn't a raving beauty, but then I'm not a hotshot stud either. But her medium size was fully and provocatively figured, and she was smart and spoke four languages and had a degree in microbiology, and my rule is to lie back in the afterglow of sufficient and highly pleasurable sex and then determine the lady's beauty rating. Don't you agree? To the last part, anyway? And her Greek is more fluent than mine, if not as comprehensive. Anyway, she had come to Greece three years before for summer vacation but also to get over the pangs of her first, and she thought probably the deepest in this life, love affair. And she had stayed in Athens with lots of trips to Mykonos, supporting herself by teaching English. She'd made a lot of Greek friends quickly, had the companionship of other Brits as well, and learned the language through singing the songs. Anyway—

Damn! I say "anyway" a lot, but every river has tributaries, and every story has asides.

So anyway, since there's still no pier in Mykonos harbor for a big boat to tie up, the little ones come out to take passengers ashore—as you know—and during being shunted to the pier, we were sort of winding down our—till then—non-stop conversation, philosophizing, "Well, life brings all sorts of things." And as we stepped ashore, bursting out of one of the little village lanes close to the pier comes this man mountain, and he grabs Judy's backpack from my hand that I had so gallantly offered to carry for her and lifts it and me off the ground, and when I come back down, he nearly knocks me over—not out of meanness, just because he needed so much room to exist. I mean, he was called *Φούσκις* (how would you translate that? The inflated one?) Of course, I had offered to carry Judy's pack because that would take me to her quarters, and since I would be tired out carrying her stuff and mine, should she not invite me up for a glass of water that would lead to sex?

This guy was an Adonis, not particularly tall, but broad in the shoulders, slim in the waste, and with rippling muscles everywhere else.

He says, "Thank you. I'll take that from here."

How else could I respond as I righted myself but to say, "You're welcome." What can a little runt seal say to a big, bad orca?

Here it comes again: anyway, as they were rushing off—no doubt but for an immediate reunion fuck—Judy turns and calls out to me, "Meet me at Madoupas tomorrow at noon; we'll play chess."

And play chess we did, with the loser buying the next round of *ouzo* and snacks, but for anything erotic, the situation looked bleak. Judy had her Adonis, a member of the national Olympic swimming team; why would she want a bantamweight like me?

She had to return to Athens the second day following for the lessons she taught at a language institute, but on leaving Mykonos, she invited me when I returned to Athens after my week on the island to go swimming with her off the rocks beyond Vouliagmeni.

I knew she lived in Anafiotika, in the Plaka, and since no one had phones, the day after I returned from Mykonos I took a chance that I'd find her and made for the very small square that was shaded by an ancient and huge tree to ask whomever I met of the locals in which little house (more like two or three small rooms) Judy lived. But there she was, sitting on the bench beside the tree's massive trunk, reading and smoking.

"I thought you might come today," she said, "so I waited. Come on, let's go. We'll walk to Syngrou and hitchhike from there."

It took us about two hours and three rides to get there—you know the place—two long curves beyond Vouliagmeni. The gradient of the cliff is shallow enough to walk down to the huge bald boulders and knuckle-like rocks that form the shore and where the sea is deep enough to dive from them. Everyone who swims there goes nude, and so did we, and we played in the water and, on land, lay touching, but innocently. I didn't harbor any plan to face down Φούσκıς to gain rutting rights with Judy. I mean, I don't have a death wish.

We returned to the Plaka, and since we hadn't eaten all day, we went to a *taverna*, where an old guy played the *santouri* for drinks and treats, and we ate cabbage salad and drank two kilos of house wine that got us fixed good—you know what I mean. I mean πολύ κέφι! And the merrier it got between us, the more I started grabbing my tensed-up biceps to judge whether they were as thick as Φούσκıς's wrists. "Surely," I said to myself over and over again, "surely, Paul, you are not so stupid as to bed the chick of a Mr. Universe." I knew that such a fine Greek lad would demand satisfaction from whoever stole his bird. "Surely. Are you? You're not," I tussled with myself.

Fortunately, Judy solved my indecision.

"Do you want to stay with me?" she asked. "I must tell you that my place is very small and humble. Might you freak out if you see it?"

"And if it were a shed or even a cave, it wouldn't bother me a bit," I answered. "But I wonder how Φούσκıς might get riled."

"Nothing to worry about; I'll tell him myself. He's coming tomorrow. And in any case, I was beginning to get bored with him. Φούσκις can have as many women as he wants."

"Obviously," I answered, "but it's one thing for a man to toss a babe and a completely different situation when another guy steals his chick."

"You are very cautious," Judy commented.

"If he were just twice my size, I would be less so."

"Don't fear. I'll tell him by myself."

Well, Jimmy, you know that bruised my male vanity—made me look cowardly—and like a complete idiot, I said, "Of course not. We'll go together."

"Bravo, Paul," Judy applauded. "Come home with me now."

Her place was really a hovel, stone age, two meters wide and three and half or so long, but neat and clean. The front door was three-quarters height—I had to bend forward to get in—and half-height to the bathroom; I had to crawl to get through it —even Judy couldn't enter standing up, even bent in half.

Just like your—well, Aliki's now—place in Piraeus, the kitchen and toilet were in the same room, separated by a side panel. And like yours, the kitchen consisted of a marble sink with a faucet for running cold water and a small counter top, and the toilet was the old hole in the ground but in a marble fixture, and it had a flushing mechanism. Everything, like I said, very neat and clean—no smells, no cobwebs, nothing damp or moldy.

For furniture, Judy had a chair and writing desk like a rostrum and a narrow bed that was also too short for me, with a mattress slightly better than stones.

But nothing cooled our enthusiasm, and we made love till first light, one on top of the other—side by side was impossible —and that's how we slept for the little time we had before the next day's reckoning with Φούσκις.

Before we set out, however, and to test whether our lovemaking was good due to the wine we had imbibed or to how well our bodies fit together, we got it on again, and it was bracing, so there was no going back. I decided—and, of course, to delay setting out—that I wanted to die clean—you know what they say, always wear clean underwear, as you might be in an accident—so I asked Judy if it were possible to take a shower.

"Sure," she said, "and now that there's two of us, nothing could be simpler."

She duck walked and entered the kitchen cum toilet, and I followed on my knees.

"Stand over the Turkish toilet and be warned: the water is cold."

And before I had time to consider how cold cold water was, she dumped a pail of it on me and said, "Soap up! No, just your head; there's shampoo on the shelf. I'll do your body."

She had a large natural sponge and a big bar of green soap, and she scrubbed me, paying more attention to some areas than others. I returned the favor, and then we rinsed off, upending pails of water on each other's head, laughing and feinting and shivering. After we dried each other and went back into the front room, we dressed. I had to wear what I had been wearing the day before, but Judy gave me a t-shirt that I insisted not be his, and because it fit, I knew it wasn't. So, I was ready, either to become a stiff or a groom, and Judy to become a one-night-stand widow or my girlfriend.

We walked to the coming field of battle, which was a store-room at the end of a stoa not far from Syntagma. In addition to Judy, as witnesses to my imminent demise were Euripides, Petros, and Aris, the Harris brothers. All were known to me and close friends with Judy. Aris, the youngest, and Φούσκις had grown up together, and they were tighter than brothers.

After the greetings, "Φούσκις," Judy said, "I've decided to live with Paul."

Needless to say, I thought she should have put a whole lot more preamble into the announcement.

"Do you have a problem with that?" she added brazenly.

There was nothing else to do but look him straight in the eyes like I had some secret weapon. I watched his facial expressions closely. He sprang from shock to rage and rushed upon me. If he caught me, I was dead, so I dodged to the side and took a fighting posture and threw a blow at his chin, but he caught my arm and pulled me through its arc to just in front of him, and then he clapped his huge arms around me, including my own hands that he had caught, and gave me a hug but not a crush. Then he whipped me around again like we were jitterbugging, grasped the open hand of the arm he held, and shook it!

"You want Judy?" he asked. "Take her with my blessing. I don't want her anymore. I found Lizzy, who has bigger tits."

"So, you are welcome, Paul, and you are welcomed," he said, and he laughed boisterously, as did the others.

Then I understood: Judy and *Φούσκις* had broken up mutually and on friendly terms on Mykonos during the trip when I'd met her, and they had arranged the whole scene that had just transpired to test my character. If I had backed off or become defensive, I probably would have been excluded from their group, but since I had attacked, I was worthy of being included. Still, that didn't make sense unless Judy had decided to have me, and the only question was when and how much fun she could have getting me.

Anyway, a few minutes later, a—I'm not sure how to describe her. She was young but regal like a queen, or as the guys called her, she was a *μπουλντόζα, Αγγλικού τύπου* (bulldozer of English type). Tall, almost chubby, but with perfect posture, and very pretty in a British way, her hair was cut in a "flappers" bob. Her cheeks shined in the cheery good health of a rose of the north. She called out in an even more upper-class English tone than Judy's, "Peter, dear, where are you?" But she didn't wait for him to answer before asking, "Peter, what is that lovely soup I liked so well yesterday called?"

Petros was in the back of the storeroom, and Aris answered for him, "*Ψαρόσουπα*, or fish soup to you."

"Pronounce that again, Ari," she said.

"*Ψωλίσουπα* (prick soup), Lillian, my love," Petros said as he came forward, interrupting Aris before he could answer.

"Okay," Lillian allowed, "but once more and slowly."

"*Ψωλίσουπα*, Lillian, *Ψωλίσουπα*," Petros replied in all seriousness.

"So wee sou pa," Lillian attempted.

"No, no," Petros said. A devil was in him. "Look, you know the word *σούπα*. *Μωρέ* (baby), *δεν έχεις Θεό* (you're unequaled). Say the English word soup and then add an 'a' at the end. Say it, *σούπα*. No, wait, just say soup."

"Soup," Lillian replied.

"Okay, good. Now add an 'a' sound to the end."

"Soupa."

25

"*Μπράβο, μωρό μου* (Good for you, my girl)," Petros said and kissed her on the cheek. Then he fondled her full melon breasts, one in each hand, and started squeezing them in rhythm. Lillian didn't try to grab or remove his hands; rather, she slapped him playfully. But Petros was not deterred and said to the assembled company, his two brothers, *Φούσκις*, Judy, and me, "See how smart my girlfriend is? She learns whatever I teach her."

To Lillian, he said, "Now you have only one more word to learn, *ψωλί* (prick), and I will say it again, *ψω λι*. Say it."

"Soy lee."

"*Όχι, όχι, βρε βλάκα* (No, no, you idiot)!" Petros shouted. "Say sew like you are sewing a button on my shirt if you ever learn to do any housework."

"Sew."

"Good, good, now put a 'p' sound in front and soften the ending: pso."

"Poe."

"No, no, my dear one, pso." Petros breathed the word as if he were blowing her a kiss.

"Psso."

"Good, you are making tremendous progress. Now, say it again but more together, pso."

"Pso," Lillian managed.

"*Μπράβο, κοπέλα μου* (Bravo, my girl)." But to us, he said, "*Να δείτε όμως ποσό γρήγορα πιάνει αλλά πράγματα* (you should see how quickly she learns other things)."

"Now you only must say lee together with pso, and you will have a new word for your vocabulary."

Lillian knows the smallest collection of Greek words any-one living in the country for three years could, even if they had tried not to learn the language. She simply speaks in English and believes that everyone should understand. She had heard the two words many times, the first when Petros ordered their meals and her favorite dish was fish, and the second when he directed her to preform his most appreciated penis manipula-tions.

"Teaching you Greek has made me tired and hungry," Pet-ros confessed. "Go to our restaurant around the corner—I have too much work to do, or I would. You will put up five fingers

26

and say your new word, *ψωλίσουπα*, and we will all eat very well."

Judy and I laughed, and when Lillian heard us, she turned her eyes more and her head slightly.

"Oh, hello, Judy. I did not notice you when I came in. How are you? And who is this?" she asked, tilting her chin towards me. "Should I order seven pso-lee-soupas instead of five, do you think?"

Just got back from three days in Arta. Jimmy, you should see this handwoven rug we bought at a nunnery where orphan girls earn part of their keep by weaving rugs on looms.

I want to finish this letter tonight and send it off tomorrow and then start one to Emerald (*Σμάραγδα*).

Back to the *Φούσκις* fiasco.

Judy, Lillian, and another young woman named Phyllis, who, at the moment, is traveling in Afghanistan, had been pals at university. The British class system is beyond my comprehension. I mean, these three women are a microcosm of social classes that only university would mix together. I have not met Phyllis yet, but she was described to me by Judy: an aristocrat with title—one she does not use, but it wouldn't have flown in our circle if she had—smart, educated toward wisdom, and a talented flute player. I am impatient to meet her when she returns from her journey.

Oh, I forgot to mention that Phyllis has been disinherited. Her family apparently disowned her hippy nature.

Lillian is new money but without the natural old-gold chic, and Judy is from the working class.

Lillian could not, or most probably would not, come to Anafiotika, and if she were not obliged, she would not even enter the Plaka—too common for her, as Judy explained. But she knew the area around Kolonaki Square well, and the interiors of the area's expensive stores. Without her man's company, however, she was loath to come to the tourist shop Petros and his brothers operated two blocks down from Syntagma.

Funny thing, I usually avoid such people, but I have come to like Lillian. The way she divides her attention is more obvious than I've ever observed in anyone else. First, she doesn't register anything mundane—I don't mean she walks out in front of buses, but whatever is not dangerous, she ignores completely. Then there are things and people of which and whom she is half-aware. I fall into that class; actually, Judy does too. If we are not talking directly to her, she forgets that we are there and expresses a languid surprise every time she rediscovers us. But finally, there are a few things—all beautiful but expensive—that she latches onto like moss, and a few people—actually, only one, Petros—on whom she is totally focused.

Judy and I departed shortly after Lillian's performance, leaving our friends to eat "prick soup" by themselves. We headed down to the flea market at Monastiraki to buy a larger bed and a better mattress. We never actually said anything, but we both, I think, just assumed that living together was, if not a good idea, a done deal. We made two trips carrying our purchases and had our first fight on the second day of our relationship. I wanted to buy a small roll-top desk, but Judy was against it for space reasons. But I had taken the measure of her place in mind and knew that the desk I'd found and could afford would indeed fit with the new and larger bed and her chair and little table and still leave a navigable path from the front door to the kitchen-bath, and even room to get down on one's knees to crawl through its passageway. I won the argument by promising to get rid of the desk if it made the space unusable. But it didn't. We found a junkman to take the old stuff. Everything of the new worked together, and we were set—shacked up, or in our case, hutted or shedded up.

It was still early afternoon of a propitious day.

Judy said, "Come, Paul, let me introduce you to my friends who live in Anafiotika." She led the way toward the upper limits of the buildings and, arriving at the first turn of the staircase, turned in the opposite direction.

"Ron!" she called out and rapped on an orange door. There was a big window with open shutters and a platform extending from its sill large enough to lie on, but there was no house, just a huge smooth-surfaced rock.

"He won't want to see anyone at first, but when his mind comes out of the clouds, he's great company. He may not even answer, although we know he's in; hear him?"

There was the tap-tap of a typewriter working.

"He's Irish, and he is writing his first novel, which he insists must live up to the standards of modern Irish literature.

I remarked that would be a difficult labor.

A booming base voice declared, "Yes, yes, I'm coming. Jud', is that you? Come in. The door's unlocked."

"Now you will see a cave made into a house if you think our place is primitive," Judy informed me.

Just an aside. When you get used to small places, big spaces are a bore. The point is, it seems to me, that one wants to be outside, in the world, not cooped up in a big house or apartment. We only use our separate quarters for private things—yeah, really private—everybody hears everyone else's pants and moans and screams of pleasure. But that's not bad. In fact, it's good so many people are getting it on; it encourages all of us.

Well, we entered, and Ron, who Judy had not described other than to say he was an Irish writer, looked both pinched like James Joyce and puffy like Dylan Thomas. He was over two meters tall and a well-knit man in general. His hair was a wild mess of orange curls. His eyes were sea-green, and his skin was the color of an unripe peach. His "house," if you could call it that, but cave-room is more accurate, fit him almost like a great cloak. He had less space than we, but surely, he needed more than the two of us. Three sides, floor, and ceiling were rock, and the fourth side was fitted with the window and ledge I had seen from outside. The door was on the shorter side of the rock and was gained by going up three rock-hewn steps.

"Ron, this is Paul," Judy said, introducing us. "He is a novelist too."

"Oh shit, another writer. Well, there's no room for more pretenders in Anafiotika."

"You mean our quota here is one, only you?" Judy asked.

"You're forgetting Jason, who's trying to become another Thomas Aquinas, and Phyllis, who's convinced she's the modern-day Shakespeare, and me, and I believe I'm the reincarnated Oscar Wilde. How many more do you want?"

"My sights are much lower," I admitted.

"Christ! And an American."

"I'm a Greek born in the U.S."

"Even worse. You probably think you're somewhere between Faulkner and Kazantzakis."

"No," I answered, "I'm just Paul."

"And humble too? That's the worst form of pride, but welcome to Anafiotika, Paul. Still, even though I'm leaving—I've almost finished my book, and I'm going to Ireland to find a publisher, you can't have my cave house. I'm keeping it during my absence to return to later and start the next work. But while I'm gone, I might allow you to come here to write. You can't believe how sitting in this nook of the Acropolis rock makes the words flow."

Our conversation with Ron centered around his claims about—actually, insistence on—the magical powers contained in but also emanating from the naked rock on the side of the Acropolis Hill, which had been given to him. He invited me to sit in the place where he wrote to allow me to feel the effect, how the rock opened the mind of the writer.

"Can you feel it?" he asked. "This rock is like a living thing that has absorbed the mysteries of the ages, and if you listen to it, it will fill you with spirits and stories."

We left Ron, and no sooner were we out of the door, down the tricky steps, and back on the path, he was tap-tap-tapping away.

"You may have been somewhat overloaded by the events of the day, your first as a resident of Anafiotika, but you must still meet Κυρία Σοφία. She's a wonderful woman who looks after all of us foreigners who live here. She even puts off the police, who occasionally check for work permits."

"Do you have one?"

"No, none of us do. Really hard to get. But the only problem so far in not having one is that every three months, I have to leave the country for at least three days. I usually go to Skopje or Brindisi, but I've gotten as far as Constantinople.

"You, as a Greek, won't have to do that."

"Right, I can stay almost a year."

"Your problem is that you can only ask from ten to fifteen drachmas per hour lesson with an American accent, whereas I charge twenty to thirty.

"Are you going to give English lessons?" she asked me.

"Certainly. My money won't last unless I work."

We had arrived at the small square that is fronted by two houses, *Κυρία Σοφία's* and John P.'s, whom I would meet later. Judy stopped at the first and called into the depths of the house through the curtains for *Κυρία Σοφία* to come out if she had a free moment to meet me.

The woman who appeared greeted Judy warmly. She was obviously a mature woman, ripened anywhere from forty to seventy. The marks of life on her face gave such a wide range to her age. She had bright and lively eyes, a smooth skin, but with deep wrinkles, and her eyebrows, which were prominent, sported many white hairs. After Judy made the introductions, *Κυρία Σοφία* evaluated me with open curiosity, and then she held out her hand to me and said, "Welcome, Pavlos, to Anafiotika; treat Judy well, and you will live pleasantly among us."

Jimmy, what can I say? Obviously, I've found a place that resonates with me, a situation that more than pleases but pleasures me. What do I win? What do I lose? In my parents' home in Hot Springs, the seven—ten if you count the kitchen-bath—square meters of living space that Judy and I share and make love and study and write and draw and cook and eat and sleep and wash and shit and completely live within would fit in the smaller closet of their guest bedroom. But the one essence that cannot fit into their big house but does in our humble abode is freedom. Looking after our material possessions takes us no time at all. Breakfast and lunch, we eat at home, mostly fresh fruits and yogurt, but for dinner, we go out with our friends to a *taverna* that sees our patronage as good advertisement to tourists, so even if we order the least expensive dishes, we get a warm welcome and super service. And the *santouri* man plays, and someone sings, and then someone else, and then all of us are singing. And flirting is ferocious but good natured. We range in size from Ron—now called Big Ron, as a little Ron and a little Ann arrived amongst us recently—to Little Anna, who is a Davida to his Goliath. And we argue about everything even when we agree with one another. And I am like a human vacuum cleaner. I'm absorbing everything I can, listening to accents and the patterns of speech, but it's so hard because I'm also always in the thick of the jabber. And I frightened the crap out of an American shithead who had been stealing books from the council library. I gave him a choice: return the books, or I would tear his eyes out. He returned the books. But I'm fearless

31

somehow over here. I even—like I told you—was willing to confront Φούσκıς over Judy. And Judy! I mean, she's three years older and has more sexual experience and is teaching me stuff every time we have sex. It's great. Last night, she pissed all over my stomach.

Look, the other thing I know is that this idyllic moment won't last long—twenty, thirty years max. You bet I intend to stretch my youth out as long as I can, but I fear that at some later time, I'll still be bouncing along while the others have settled down. Sure, there will be new friends to make, but the old ones are one's mirror.

I've been trying to figure out how to say it, to wish my parents well and hope they enjoy the results of their labor but demand that they leave me alone. You know how, sometimes, when you're kind of off in another world and your mind's defenses are down and, all of a sudden, a scene—pictures, sounds—pops into your attention. When that happens to me, the condensed drama is always Mother muttering, "Παναγιά (Mother of God), how can I set him straight? Show me the way." I'm her averaged-out idiot-savant son.

Imagine not having to hear her entreaties to the higher powers about fixing me. Sound is sweet again!

And look, I've lived that life. Sure, I'm immature, but I'm not stupid either. I see what they go through to be successes in business and the community, how much they consider what other people might think about a myriad of subjects. These other people are no wiser than they, but they allow, or even invite, them to change their attitudes and behavior. And how they're always smiling but never happy. I know all that stuff, all right! But no one has ever been able to explain to me why anyone should spend and bend their youth and prime to work and routine. See, Jimmy, I know that I have been very fortunate—I haven't lived through war and occupation, haven't starved or not had a warm home. No one has abused me. In fact, it's been the opposite; I've been pampered. But do you see what that does to you—did to me—when you finally meet strong people who are in all the ways I've observed better than I am, more real, solid men and women who have had few if any of my advantages but have turned out stronger for all their deprivations. I want to be real. I want to have to think about every day, to take nothing for granted, to live as though everything has to be earned always, to have no expectations, to never be a special case.

Look, I'm directing this to Emerald as well; my hope is that you two will exchange letters so that those I write to each of you can be completely different.

Shit, if there was one thing that could have held me back, it was Emerald's plight. If I could have done anything, I might have—no, probably would have—stayed to help her. Her father was half-crazed with daughter-directed desire when she turned from girl to woman: a mother who appeased the father while protecting the daughter, and the daughter (you, Emerald, if you read this) being ground out of her gentle and creative nature and her aptitude for mathematics. The young girl I grew up with, who had the twinkliest eyes that have ever enlivened a face, was dulled down to an almost zombie state to be sold into marriage to a man who promised her father not to touch her or let anyone else approach her so that she could remain the vir- ginal woman-girl siren of his desires. A community divided be- tween the shame of divorce and the pain of marriage. And then there is Stavros himself, who, Emerald, I believe is a victim as much as you. I admit there are places in rural Greece that don't hold women's rights or desires in high regard. As you know only too well, your father was a native of such a backward vil- lage. I was pleased when I heard that your dad was bringing you back to meet your roots. I thought it would be as inspiring to you as that experience had been and still is to me. Little did anyone imagine, and you probably least of all, that your dad had gone over the fence. I think that when you turned into a woman, you floored him—him? Hell! All of us. I mean, lady, you are a looker with extreme intelligence, and your eyes, lady, are another universe. Not many men can measure up to your standards—I never felt I could. But here's my problem with you now. I grant that you walked into a horrible situation blind- folded by the encouragement of your father. But you don't have to say yes; you didn't have to put on the wedding dress and march down the aisle. You could have said no, and you could have ripped up the dress. Maybe I'm off base. Jimmy, what do you say? A child cannot allow a parent to rule its adult life. Bad enough the crap—the norms of a stinking society—they feed us before we can get away. And it's not even a current society but the remains of distant ancestors! Sorry, I know that you, Emerald, are the most aggrieved victim, but I can't help thinking of Stavros too. A sixty-year-old man, widower for thirty, is offered a nearly nineteen-year-old beauty with brains and a ticket to the U.S., and in return, all he has to do is promise not to approach her sexually and keep everyone else at bay. He would have needed to be a very wise man to see the impossibility and the unsuitability of the match and the offer.

I'll say more in my letter to you, Emerald, but believe me—and Jimmy will confirm this—that both he and care I for you and want only the best for you, and believe us, you deserve it.

Right, Jimmy?

Anyway, to finish the introduction of Judy. I felt and still feel that I had lived or learned about 90% of what the normal world offered and demanded. I wanted and want something different, and I believe I've discovered the first steps here in Anafiotika with Judy. We agreed at the beginning that we would share expenses half and half. Her rent is forty drachmas per month, i.e., $1.34. Food is cheap—a large loaf of whole-grain bread costs two cents. I've got clothes. My studies at the university are free except for books. Ahead, there seems to be a world of possibilities that require little time lost on work for pay to explore.

Jimmy, I'm set. Please try to explain what I mean and intend to my parents. Emerald, please help him.

The decision came to me after meeting Κυρία Σόφια. She had sized me up and found me suitable to join Anafiotika. And I saw in her and the neighborhood the bedrock of a new reality.

As we left Κυρία Σόφια, Judy asked, "Are you hungry and want to go to our restaurant, or should we go home and try out how well our new furniture holds us?"

I answered, "I'm hungry, but for you, not for food."

And she said, "My dear Paul, I think we will get on well."

3: WATER, WATER EVERYWHERE

Jane and Mary shared a stateroom on a freighter that accepted twelve passengers. They departed New Orleans for the port of Tunis, and then zigged up to Naples, and then zagged down to Alexandria, and then shunted over to Haifa, and finally zigged back to Piraeus, a passage of twenty-nine days of sailing and eight days at ports of call for a total of thirty-seven in all.

Their ship, the *Panagia* (Mother of God, a designation that pleased them both), flew the Greek flag and served Mediterranean cuisine and delicious food, and the captain conducted an Orthodox lay service every Sunday and Wednesday, and they sang in his choir. What more could they ask for?

Possibly, for separate cabins, but they managed somehow to work out the two-women-in-one-smallish-space problem. They had been close friends for years, so personality traits were not in contention. On Mary's side, she was obliged to listen to Jane's interminable outlining, defining, exaggerating the proper and best course for Paul's future. On Jane's, Mary snored loudly all night in rapturous bursts.

There was a grain of justice in their trade-off, and presumably, they realized it.

Before meeting John and Jane in 1947, occasioned by the coincidence of Paul's family's move to Hot Springs while Mary was healing in the city during a month's long course of thermal mineral baths, Mary had known Jane's mother and Jane herself as a child, even as a young woman, and her two older sisters and three younger brothers as well. She had lost contact when Jane's mother, Maria, had relocated the family from Joliet to Peoria.

Jane was a grown baby, an innocent of life. She had gone from her father's home to her husband's without ever being solely responsible for herself, and she was thereby spoiled. But the dimensions of her need for special status included constant support and reassurance that John supplied unobtrusively, but when John was absent, Jane was adrift.

Mary had learned personal independence from an early age, and she understood each person's desire to live as they wished, and each person's pain and guilt in conforming to societal norms and enforced conditions that were often antithetical to their predilections. The progress of Mary's experience from the beginning of her memory, her long convalescences interfering too often in her desperate struggle to keep her business afloat to provide herself with occupation and sustenance, and the constant pain she bore in her shattered legs that never completely healed had taught her to see life as a play, her personal history as a role. Each grounded person was both in the audience and on the stage, but Jane was aware only of the director's privilege.

Mary was also a poet; she wrote in Greek and showed no one her work, which, over the years, became a large opus. She knew her vision would anger others because it drew the world and life in different pictures than most people sought and held.

Her marriage had not been successful, but in comparison to what? To an ideal union, but would everyone agree to the same paragon?

At least matrimony had transported her from a devastated and impoverished island to a wealthy nation that had given her a new chance and direction in life.

Wasn't there a trade-off in everything, as in the saying "You can't have the dog full and the pie whole"?

Jane was one who thought you could, believed, in fact, that having a surfeit of goods and especially services was her right. But Jane wasn't at fault for that attitude; her mother was. But Maria, Jane's mother, was not at fault either; her mother was, and on and on, the misconception tumbled, back to original sin.

Nothing was certain, or put the other way, everything was uncertain. How could people not see that? No one had a right to anything even though they all had a responsibility for everything.

Back on Syros, where Jane had been born in 1912—although she often claimed Joliet in 1916, when the family arrived in the U.S. and she was almost five—her father, George, had been a baker, and a good one; he had been appointed as a "king's baker" in Greece, enabling him to mark his wares with a miniaturized stamp of the official medallion, the ultimate accolade for a commoner and an acknowledgment of his excellence in the profession, and he, in turn, was a fervent monarchist. But then the English navy blockaded Syros, and the stores of wheat were severely rationed: one loaf per family regardless the number of children.

Women, mothers, had scratched and pawed at the door of his bakery, crying, moaning, entreating, "Please, please, Mr. George, give me another loaf of bread—whatever you have; my children are hungry, and I have so many."

His position was untenable, intolerable; if he disobeyed the directive and gave additional loaves to those most needy, he would be arrested for sedition, but if he didn't, his gentle, ethical nature would be destroyed and him along with it. At the breaking point of his crisis, a letter arrived after months of delay from his wife's brothers in Cairo, who had opened a confectionery that was doing very well. They wanted George to come to Egypt and bring his family and become their baker. And in 1915, George and his wife, Maria, midterm pregnant, their three daughters—Jane the youngest of them, not quite three years old—and their eldest son, John, made the dangerous journey from Piraeus to Alexandria; German U-boats were hunting.

That adventure lasted less than two years, as Maria's brothers employed her husband and paid him well but refused to take him in as a partner, whereas they give her, their sister, a silent share. That became a crisis in George's spirit as well, one of a different sort, but unbearable just the same. As a consequence, in November of 1916, he and his family, still three daughters but now with two sons, returned to Alexandria and sailed, again perilously, to New York.

The Hellenic king's bakers were, or should have been, either sole proprietors or at least equal partners.

Maria, however, had wanted to stay in Egypt; her brothers were there, while she knew no one in the U.S. In Cairo, as well as in Alexandria, a large Greek community lived in perfect peace and harmony with the Egyptians. The two ethnicities were more rather than less similar, and that was not what she had heard about America, especially Chicago, which was close to Joliet, their destination.

As a good wife, she would follow her husband if she couldn't steer him, but she wasn't disposed to like his decisions.

On the steamer, as each piece of the children's clothing became soiled, Maria tossed it overboard along with her own and her husband's, leaving a link—firm in her mind no matter how ephemeral in fact—to home, back to Egypt if not to Greece. They would all arrive at their new country in their last and best set of clothes, which would be thrown into the harbor at the first opportunity.

The ship had docked at the port of New York; the family disembarked to begin the refugee reception process. When called forward to the registrar's counter, George handed over their passports and responded to the clerk's question with his name, age, and need, or not, of immediate medical attention.

Having finished with George, the clerk turned to Maria. "What is your name?" he asked.

She did not respond.

The clerk repeated his question.

Again, she refused to answer.

Then George nudged her and said in Greek, "You know how to answer. Give him your name."

Maria was unmoved.

The clerk was becoming impatient. George worried, while the children were clueless except for the eldest daughter, Francis, who also urged her mother to speak.

Maria remained mum.

"Are you going to answer?" the clerk demanded.

Nothing, no reply. Finally, Francis understood the reason, and she turned and, speaking English for the first time out of a classroom, said, "Politely, please."

And the clerk, on the chance that an unpleasant situation might be avoided, asked again but diffidently, "Madam, please tell me you name."

This time, she replied, "Maria Argoudeli."

38

And the family, because it looked clean and fit, was admitted to America and would eventually take citizenship.

Yet, for all the obvious benefits of the nation, Maria became unhappy with her life in such a frenzied society, and the longer she lived in the U.S., the more despondent she became, and as a result, she refused to learn English.

It was an impolite tongue; if not the language, then the people who spoke it were.

Mary Pappas sympathized with Maria, but she had not enjoyed the same choice; she had been compelled by circumstances to learn English well. Her accent was heavy, but her vocabulary was extensive, and—in comparison to Greek—grammar and syntax were obvious to her. True, some of the spelling was weird, but she mastered the oddities quickly. In fact, she spoke English to Jane, whose Greek was bounded; but Mary preferred speaking in Greek, especially with John, who still used the old and polite expressions.

And she had sympathized with Maria also on the burden of living under constant discrimination. Except for the Native Americans, who were treated even worse, all Americans were immigrants, but many willfully filled themselves with, and freely expressed, xenophobia against new arrivals after only a single generation of native birth, and some didn't even wait for their children's rant.

Greeks were generally held in low regard, possibly because they would do the hardest, often lowest-paid and dirtiest work and make the necessary sacrifices until they saved enough capital to start their own business and then rapidly became comparatively wealthy.

Maria's solution to the stifling environment was simple: she ignored the barbarians and taught her children to think and act like Greeks, and she ran her household as if the world was divided into us and them, the non-Greeks, whom she called foreigners in their own land; they were not worth knowing. She filled her children with pride, insured that all of them learned Greek and spoke it exclusively within the home, curtailed their contact with outsiders, and maintained a propriety in living that eliminated all the laxity and freedom of the American way but precluded the discriminating locals from finding fault in any of them for any reason.

Her daughters were her eldest children, and she dedicated their youth to securing an early and appropriate marriage. As part of their training to become proper mothers, Maria assigned to each of them a son to look after. To the brothers, the care of the sisters was bliss for the attention and leisure it gave them, and hell for the inspection and coercion they were under to be good.

When she was twenty-two, Francis was married by arrangement to a man twice her age; still, he had his own business.

Helen, the middle daughter, didn't want wedded bliss at all, preferring to retain the aloof princess librarian mode of life, but she was compelled to make way for Jane, and she married the least suitable man for her type because he was brash enough to compliment her beauty and thus made her a victim of her own mother-inspired vanity.

George had taken his eldest son, Argi, to Egypt as a companion and for the educational exposure to a different culture immediately after Helen's wedding, promising to return in time for Jane's. He had decided to expand his bakery to compete with the bread factories that were arising in the culture of mass production and stealing his business. His own finances were insufficient to fund the modernization, and banks were not interested—if they were still operating in 1935 after the crash of '29—to lend to an independent baker in view of the developing trend. Thus, he had decided to sell Maria's share in the Cairo confectionery; the business had prospered so well that the brothers had opened branches in all the major Egyptian cities. George's brothers-in-law had been agreeable to buy back the share that they had given in a moment of weakness and generosity, but he was obliged to travel to Egypt to close the transaction, as they were unable to export such a large sum of foreign currency, i.e., dollars.

Mary's contact with George and Maria's family lessened as her mobility deceased and her direct knowledge of their doings become scanty and second-hand. She had heard of the tragedy—everyone in the Greek community had. George had sold Maria's share for $75,000, a veritable fortune in those days, but either when he arrived home or along the return journey, disaster had struck.

Jane wanted to be a June bride, but only the last two Sundays of the month were possible dates. The first Sunday, the 6th, was too soon for her father's return; no one wanted to be conjoined on the 13th of any month, leaving the 20th and 27th as possible days. George and Argi were slated to return on the 18th, and so Jane chose the 20th of June, 1937.

The household was in the usual prenuptial commotion; George and Argi's arrival only added another level of ruckus in the family circle, and the disappearance of the fifteen $5,000 American Express checks from the sale of Maria's share was not discovered until Monday.

Jane and John knew nothing of the loss, as they had set off immediately after the reception to drive to Niagara Falls.

When the loss of the checks was established, George suffered a panic attack and fell into an almost catatonic state.

As the checks were American Express instruments, after reporting their loss and check numbers, and if they had not already been cashed, the money would be reissued, but only after a lengthy process. It was salvation and catastrophe in one: the money would be recovered, but now it would be taxed and at a punishingly high rate, and George would be fined, if not worse, for failing to report the importation of a large sum.

His health never recovered even though the money minus taxes and fines was eventually reimbursed, and within six months, he died from lingering shock, increasing depression, and soaring incredulity. After George's death, Maria moved to Peoria from Joliet; she liked her two sons-in-law there, who both had businesses that were better than the one owned by the son-in-law in Joliet, who didn't seem to work at anything yet always had an unbelievable wad of money carried in his right front trouser pocket, like a Chicago bank roll but with a difference. Instead of a twenty wrapped around ones, his was a sawbuck note covering fifties beneath. But his family commitment was deplorable; he never returned home before the small morning hours, and then he was always drunk and randy.

The randy part was the wreck of mother-daughter consultation; Maria refused to talk about so vile a subject as a woman's role in sex, which God—or at least the Church—had ordained should only be engaged in for procreation, and no one had convinced her otherwise. Helen couldn't drive (three-hundred-mile round trip), there were no direct trains, and none of the buses were express, her husband disliked his mother-in-law as much as she detested him, there was always the telephone, but Maria quickly developed hearing problems, and thus she could live unamused by her daughter's troubles but also unabused by them in Peoria while Helen gritted her teeth in Joliet. Hadn't she warned her middle daughter not to marry for vanity, especially as there had been more vetted suitors who had desired her, men with more decorum who had not ogled and complimented only her physical characteristics, but rather admired her for her aristocratic bearing and sharp mind. Indeed, Helen had been placed in a no-win situation; she hadn't wanted to marry anyone but had been compelled to make a choice. She'd already reached the age of twenty-four and, thus, had been pushing spinsterhood. Plus, Helen—unequal to the reactions that would condemn the lifestyle she wished to lead—had needed to accept an offer, just not the one she had, and get out of Jane's way (the youngest daughter of any proper family, and certainly hers, could not marry until all the older ones had).

Paul was born two years and a month later, the heaviest and largest birth of the year at Memorial Hospital.

* * *

"If only Paul would listen," Jane was saying for the thousandth time at least.

Mary looked away from her friend and removed her sunglasses to look up into the light blue sky that was veiled by a vast semitransparent sheet of high clouds. She had never seen a circular rainbow before. No, not a rainbow but a halo centered on the sun that was diffused into a core of very bright white light about which streamed two sets of rings of rainbow colors. The outer color bands were wider and fainter than the inner, and at the furthest boundary of the second and last blue band was another one, very wide and delicately rose tinted, that faded into the clear sky beyond its maximum extent.

"Look, Jane, look," she said and pointed toward the vision miracle.

And Jane did glance up briefly. "Pretty," she said and then resumed her complaining posture, staring at her hands folded in her lap when she was imagining what she hoped were the narrow limits of Paul's indiscretions, staring directly at Mary when she expected enlightenment, or at least encouragement, and occasionally closing her eyes and tilting her face toward heaven when she was imploring divine intervention, which, when it appeared, she merely called "pretty."

"If only," Jane began again.

Mary cut her off; the vision of the sun halo had given her inspiration. "I just thought of something you could do, Jane. But listen to me before you react."

"I always listen."

"No, you don't; you have an opinion before you've heard the full statement."

"No, I don'ts" and "yes, you dos" passed back and forth a number of times until Mary, becoming exasperated, broke the cycle and said, "As you wish, but listen to me now and don't say anything until I've finished.

"What if you were to suggest to Paul that if he loves the woman enough to live with her, why not marry her? It's—"

Jane could hear no more, nor contain herself, and she barked, "Mary, what are you suggesting? That he marry the s-l-u-t!"

"You don't know the circumstances; I don't think it's fair to call her that."

"What else could she be? Don't you see—"

"No, I don't see, Jane. Paul has not done any of the things you fear yet, and if you handle him correctly, he won't

"What do you mean? I've been writing him continuously. It's so hard to get him on the telephone I've stopped trying."

"And if he were here and you were talking to him face to face, what would you say?"

"I'd tell him—"

"But that is your biggest problem, Jane. You would *tell* him. He is not going to listen. He wants to grow up and be his own man."

"But he hasn't yet, and maybe he can't ever."

"Exactly! If he had, he would not be so aggressive."

"What are you suggesting?

"Reverse psychology."

"Meaning?"

"You suggest to the person you are trying to influence the exact opposite of what you really want them to do."

"And how would that help, especially in Paul's case?"

"If you phrase it as a question encouraging the very thing the other person thinks they want, but you don't, they relax and stop objecting to what you are saying."

"And that would be?"

"What I said. You would avoid confrontation completely if possible, and when the two of you are alone and relaxed because you haven't been arguing about anything, you could say something like, 'Paul, if you love Judy enough to live with her, wouldn't it be better to be married? Don't you think Judy would prefer to be accepted as your wife?'"

"And that would serve what purpose?"

"Scare the pants off him."

"How?"

"Don't you see? This is probably the first time that he has lived with a woman."

"I'm not sure about that. There were at least two indications that something of that nature was going on when he was at Northwestern."

"Well, not this openly at least. But the deeper truth is, I think, that he's practicing with the female."

"Why do you say that?"

"Because she is older than he, and as you have said many times, there are some very lovely Greek girls who are younger and virgins. Can you believe how beautiful Emerald has become? She changed from a girl to woman in just a few months' time. I watched it happening and could not believe my eyes."

"I know, but what a shame her fathered married her off—"

"You mean forced her to marry."

"—to Stavros. What a horrible deed; why, it's even worse than Paul marrying that English woman."

"The point is that virginity becomes very important to men when they are considering a wife. If you suggest the serious step of marriage, he will probably move out immediately."

"You don't know Paul; that could be dangerous."

"Not as well as you, obviously, but I do know that he wants respect from his parents just as anyone wants the good regard of others. So, if you state the question correctly and stay on mark for any following discussion, you can transfer all the burden of decision to him because you are no longer acting the mother but have become the disinterested friend. Once Paul realizes and feels that the decision is on him alone, and that you and John will be happy with whatever he decides to do, he will think differently. He does not want to settle down yet; I'm sure of it. He knows he has military service in front of him, and the army is no place to have a wife if you're not a professional. Plus, obviously, he wants more schooling, and again, a wife would just be a diversion from his studies."

"Do you think that would work?"

"I cannot guarantee that you will get the desired result, but consider that you have not been able to change his mind with any other argument you have ever used."

Mary was right Jane conceeded. The relationship between her son and herself had deteriorated. She could feel Paul's intent to act against her, all of her wishes, automatically it seemed.

For the first time that day, as they had been sitting in lounge chairs on the freighter's small observation deck, she began to relax. What Mary was saying actually made sense. Jane had resisted the idea, but eventually, she understood that she often drove Paul to do something by trying to prevent him from doing it.

She loved her son in her way, but surpassing affection, there was duty that came packaged with opportunity, and Paul was their only child and, thus, the foundation of the commercial fiefdom that she and John wanted to create for and bequeath to him, and through him to their many grandchildren who were waiting to be conceived. But Paul was a wounded man, not quite right—even he knew that—and she and John had to keep him close to protect him, as she had failed to do at the life changing moment of his accident.

Maybe reverse psychology would work. She had always been too direct with Paul, keeping things simple, as she was forced to do after the accident, but she had not changed her approach as quickly as he had overcome its effects. She needed to become not more mature with him—he was not ready for that yet—but more coy. Was it worth a try? But as Mary had said, everything else she had attempted in the past had failed to wake Paul up.

She looked out over the sea; it was calm, and the ship hardly rolled. The sun's halo had been pretty, beautiful, in fact, and she looked for it again, but its moment had passed.

4: TRIAL BY MARRIAGE

She was dear to him, but Emerald was younger and much brighter than Paul, and he had been shy and awkward with her, and now that she was approaching her eighteenth birthday and independence through achieving the age of majority, she had been forcibly married to an old man.

Old? sixty at least.

Emerald had been the first local child Paul had met when his family had moved to Hot Springs, Arkansas, in 1946. Her father, George, owned an old-fashioned candy store, and his specialty was New Orleans-style pralines. That they were delicious, Paul would vouch.

The Illinois Candy Co., moreover, occupied the street level front section of the building that continued sixty meters up the gentle slope of the mountainside to the rear section that housed the Virginia Apartments where Mary had lived, and it was on the corner fronting Central Avenue and across Canyon Street from the DeSoto Hotel, which would become Paul's nemesis.

Paul had been seven going on eight, while Emerald had been three going on four. She'd been a bright, active child with shining silver-gray eyes; he'd been a dull, listless kid trying to figure out the simplest things all over again, and again.

* * *

Paul's letter read:

> Dearest Emerald,
>   I cannot express the depth of my agitation upon learning of your marriage. Why did you do it?

Just months ago, when I learned that you and your father were coming to Greece, I was really happy. I planned to take you all over Athens and show you the sights tourists seldom see, and to introduce you to a group of remarkable—I think—characters who are my friends and neighbors in Anafiotika, a special part of Plaka.

Jimmy warned me, but not you, that he feared an unpleasant surprise awaited you in Greece from a comment that your dad made at a church party while you were dancing, leading the circle. He was scrutinizing your rhythmic figure, and Jimmy heard him say beneath the noise in the hall, music, and voices, "If I can't have her, nobody will."

Jimmy was about to reply, but decided against it, hoping that your dad's thought was a passing one, or that he did not mean what it meant. I suggested that he tell you, but he didn't agree. Did he finally?

From different sources, Jimmy mainly, but also my mother and Mary, I learned what happened. Your father whisked you off to his native village, and remote villages are just that, remote. After I learned what it is called, I couldn't even find it on my map!

When I first went to Mykonos years ago, I saw a way of life that had changed little over hundreds of years, and mind you, Mykonos had been designated to become a tourist attraction. It metamorphosed fast, but your dad's village has not experienced that influence.

They told me that he didn't allow you personal money. Surely, that was a warning sign. Did they browbeat you, or worse?

But if they didn't hold your feet to the fire, I can't understand why you would choose to marry an old widowed peasant rather than go to university on the IBM scholarship you won. The company only gives fifty in the whole country!

Please write back and tell me the straight story and also if I can be of any use in untangling you. But enough; letters shouldn't be bitchy, and this one has been.

I'll continue with funnier stuff.

First, Anafiotika; it's like an island village—nothing like your dad's—in the heart of Athens. The story goes that builders from the Cycladic island Anafi came to Athens to work in construction. They needed a place to live and were allowed to build a copy of their home village on the slope of the Acropolis.

I'll enclose a picture of our village center; it's a small—tiny —square shaded and domed by an ancient tree at the base of which are a few tables and chairs, and a couple of benches.

Of an evening, some number of us congregate there for neighbor-talk. We are locals and foreigners of which the British are the plurality, but all the others speak English well as a second language. Of our widely different characteristics, still Hakim and Sue stand out, Hakim because he is a walking bundle of joy and nonsense, seeding happiness wherever he goes, Sue, because she is an innocent, like a flower's perfume that fills the ether with an aroma of pungent sexuality.

I said the foreigners all speak English, but I must make an exception for Hakim, who speaks Hakimian. He's West Indian or Jamaican, and a Rastafarian, and he mixes deep argot with a slippery mix of English-Spanish-French and speaks in short bursts that no one fully understands but that make everyone laugh. His skin color is so black they could use him at the national bureau of standards to define the color, but in the mist of his light-hoarding pigmentation are the flashing, almost always pink to red, whites of the eyes and dazzling white teeth in a large and mobile mouth. He wears dreadlocks tied to bone wickets on the outside to stick straight up on the inside of the bundle, and in the middle of what looks like a head-mounted personal volcano, there is indeed a crater where he keeps his marijuana and smoking paraphernalia.

He and Sue have two children that are a perfect milk-chocolate in complexion. The family has as much money as the dope that's left to sell after Hakim takes his stash. Getting high is a religious ritual for him, but we all join in the trip.

Gotta go. Write soon.

Love, Paul

* * *

"I have no money, but I can give you this," a small, thin man dressed in a cheap, ill-fitting ocher-colored suit said to Paul. "It's very valuable and beautiful," he added.

"What?" Paul asked, startled. He had been reading, sitting on the bench before the tree in the petite square of Anafiotika, lost to the outside.

"I must learn American English," the man continued, "and to sound like an American."

"Wait a minute," Paul demanded, trying to get on the same page as reality. "Why tell me?"

"You teach."

"How do you know that?" Paul was surprised. He had gotten students through other teachers whose pupils' friends also wanted lessons, but the circle was tight, and the fact closely held. Lack of work permits meant that trouble with the police was always possible, though not as dire for Paul as for the others because the authorities didn't worry much about a foreign Greek, even one working illegally.

"I'm in the police, and I have your file. Also the woman's."

"Judy's?"

"Yes, that is the given name."

"Wow," Paul said. "And do you have files on others as well?"

"Yes, all of you."

"I thought we were undetected.'

"No, very obvious."

"You mean to everyone?"

"No, just to the police; no one else cares."

"So, I don't understand. You've come to arrest me if I agree to take your payment, whatever it is, in exchange for English lessons?"

"No, to arrange for lessons. English is necessary to my career."

"Now I'm even more confused," Paul objected. Before he continued, he opened the small box the man had handed to him. In it, he found a cameo the size of a half-dollar coin depicting a female. Holding the jewelry in one hand and pointing with the other, Paul said, "Yes, it's very beautiful. Who is it?"

"Sappho," the man answered. "The piece is from the fourth century BC."

"You mean it's original?"

"It is."

"And you want me to accept this ancient cameo in return for giving you lessons in American English? Isn't that illegal for both of us?"

"Yes," the man responded.

"Yes to what? Both questions?"

"Yes."

"Ah," Paul said, stalling. "Sorry, somehow I feel like I'm about to step into a trap here. I mean, if this cameo is authentic, I could be charged with stealing, or at least unauthorized possession of an ancient antiquity."

"You could. I would not give it if I had another choice. You would have to make me Shakespeare to earn its worth."

"Christ!" Paul exclaimed. He had graduated from "Wow."

"Look, most people want to learn a British accent. Why . . ."

"I can't tell you that, not yet."

The cameo was indeed beautiful, and Paul was sorely tempted to teach the policeman, but the implications were unforeseeable.

"What kind and level of lessons do you want?" Paul asked.

"Conversation at a high level."

"Grammar, syntax?"

"I know Greek," the man answered.

"Right," Paul acknowledged. "Look," he went on, "what if you give me this as a gift, not a payment, and we talk as friends, not as student/teacher."

"I want full lessons, not a few minutes, and hard ones."

"I have an idea," Paul said. "First, show me identification so that I know you are really a police officer."

"You must take my word."

"Ah." Paul's idea was falling apart before it could be tested.

"All right," Paul conceded; there was potentially too much adventure in this offer to be refused. "Then I suggest you take me with you on your investigations, and we'll speak in English about every aspect."

"It could be dangerous."

"Not a problem," Paul answered as if he meant it.

"When can we start? Oh, my name is Pavlos."

"So is mine!"

"I know, but we call you Paul."

"When do you want to start? Now? Are you headed off somewhere for policework?"

"Yes."

"I have to begin asking you single questions," Paul said in English. "Where to?"

"This is good English, 'where to'?"

"No, but it is colloquial."

"Colloquial?" Pavlos asked.

"It's from the Latin, colloquium, I think, and it means expressions in daily use, like demotic phrases in Greek."

"Them we go to Monastiraki to see a friend and informer," Pavlos revealed.

"Who are we after?" Paul asked.

"Communists," Pavlos answered.

"What's wrong with communists?" Paul inquired, not expecting the answer he heard.

"Nothing. It is only the normal nonsense of a state needing an enemy. Before, it was the fascists. Now it's the communists. Tomorrow it will be the anarchists or the socialists or the atheists or whoever is handy and making a nuisance of themselves."

"Are you going to arrest someone?"

"No, only keeping records."

"Of what? Movements, friends—that sort of thing?"

"Yes. It is the same for all, including foreigners. Everybody has a record. There may be nothing in it, but it's there waiting for the first piece of information. The only people we do not have records on are those who are about to commit a crime. That is, we probably have the records, but they are in the wrong file, or one that can't be found."

"I see," Paul said.

"No, you don't. You accept it as real, but it is not. It is all made up. If it were not, how would people like me live, or soldiers, or politicians, or priests? The system is made to be complicated so that many people can be involved in running it, and that allows many people to steal from it."

"Like the cameo," Paul taunted.

"No, I did not steal it. I found it but did not turn it in. If I had, my superior would have taken it home for his wife."

"Would you call that corruption?" Paul asked, testing how far he could prod Pavlos.

"You could, but that tells you no thing."

"You want to say nothing, not no thing."

"The word 'corruption' tells you nothing, then; much better to say that human nature is in conflict with human nature."

Paul was thinking about Pavlos's statement as they arrived at the first contact point. It was a re-tinning workshop, and they were greeted by a figure sitting in back wearing an apron and heating a large copper kettle with a gas torch. All around him and scattered through the workshop were copper utensils colored by various stages of oxidation and thinning or completely worn away tin cladding.

"Who is this?" the man asked.

"My English teacher," Pavlos answered.

"So, you finally found an American?"

"Finding Americans is not hard," Pavlos explained, "but finding one who will give language conversation lessons and accept a small gift for payment is."

"You won't change your mind?" the tinsmith asked.

"No, I must go."

"To the U.S.?" Paul asked.

"Every year, soldiers and police officers go there for training. The exam is hard; I already sat for it once but was not selected because my skills in English were not good enough. I can retake the exam but only once, and I intend to sit for it in two months."

"How long will you be there for training?"

"I do not intend to return; I will find a woman to marry and stay."

"Pavlos," Paul began, "I understand, and I do not understand. I was born in the country, but I do not fit there."

"Ah, that is a privilege few people have."

"What is?"

"To be able to ask whether you like the place where you must live. Few people in the world can. Most of us are stuck where we are born. Bombs may be falling and bullets flying, or there is no work, or what people produce may not feed them well, or at all. But if conditions are such that you must leave, where can you go? Who wants a displaced person?

"Was it your father or grandfather?" Pavlos asked.

"Father."

"And how did he go?"

"Before restrictive laws were passed in the early 1920s, it was much easier to enter. My father was a sailor, and he debarked in '21 and registered his entry into the country at the New York docks for five dollars and had his name shortened in the bargain."

"Now it is much harder, and if you try to go the legal way, it's almost impossible."

"I see," Paul confirmed. "You will jump school, not ship."

"What does this mean?" Pavlos asked.

"Illegal entry into the country was often done by sailors failing to return to their ships after shore leave, and so they called it 'jumping ship,' but your ship will be the training facility, and so you will 'jump school.'"

"I see," Pavlos allowed, and then he asked, "Your father was happy with his decision to remain?"

"Delirious!"

"Delirious?"

"Exceedingly happy, but... There's always a but, isn't there? When I found out a couple of years ago when we returned as a family, me for the first time, my dad after thirty-five years, and my mother even longer, that he had never taken American citizenship, it really shocked me. He is a man who professes admiration for the American Way, and yet he did not become a citizen. He voted, but how he did that, I can only guess. He must have gotten into the system early, and once in, they had voting cards like identification, he stayed in. The last thing I would have believed was that my father didn't become a citizen immediately. Why did he wait thirty-five years and then take citizenship in order to get a passport to come back to Greece?"

"Didn't you ask him?"

"I did, but his answer was a hem haw, and that means indecisive."

"If I get there, I will not come back," Pavlos announced, "but like your father, Greece will always be in my heart."

"Then why go?"

Instead of answering, Pavlos turned to the tinsmith and said, "Still on for tonight?"

"Yes," the man answered.

"What's on?" Paul asked as if he had a right to know.

"One reason why I will not come back. We will round up communists tonight. They are planning a demonstration that will not be allowed to happen. But we"—Pavlos indicated himself and his friend—"agree with their demands. Doesn't matter. They will be arrested with our help. It is all part of the game. To control a person, make him afraid, no different than with a country: make the citizens afraid of enemies within and without."

"You agree with the communists, but you are in the police in a country where their party is not legal?"

"Yes."

"And after you arrest them, what happens?"

"Stop their demonstration, put them in jail, maybe make them hurt."

"You mean torture them?"

"Yes. Not too much bad. No one dies."

Paul did not correct the syntax, but rather responded with one of his standards: "Wow."

"Do you want to see?"

"Yes," Paul answered without thinking.

"The *caffenion* on the corner of Omonia Square and Piraeus Avenue at eleven o'clock. Stay across the street if you don't want to be taken in the sweep. If you do, play backgammon at an inside table."

When Pavlos and his tinsmith friend went for coffee, the lesson was over, but they had arranged for further meetings. Paul hurried back to Anafiotika to find Judy and enlist her in the adventure of getting arrested.

* * *

"I hope we are not about to get into a lot of trouble we don't need," Judy opined. "Are we being recklessly stupid?"

"Look, they've already got files on us; they know who we are, where we live, and that we live together and teach English. If they wanted us, they have us, but this is a rare chance for us to see the other side of the country. We live in one Greece, and the Greeks live in another. You and I see a lot of the other, the real side, because we speak the language and have many friends, but this is different. If it goes like Pavlos hinted it will, we'll see into one of society's cracks, the political divisions between hard left and hard right. I haven't seen that deeply into American society; have you into the English?"

"No," Judy admitted. "After the war, in school and later university, my world was tightly closed in upon itself. I paid little attention to political happenings because they didn't seem to affect me. I suppose if the government suddenly had decided to charge tuition at university, we students probably would have organized and demonstrated and done whatever people with a beef do."

"I misspoke," Paul interjected.

"Ha," Judy exclaimed, "double six!"

They had begun their game, and she had rolled the first die. Her choices were to put four chips on the seven slot of her outer broad, or two chips on the thirteen slot of Paul's outer board or one chip on his inner board nineteen slot. That would be a gutsy move. If he rolled double fives or a five and anything, or a two and a three, or a four and a one, he would nail her. But Judy was a crafty player, and getting nailed on the second move of the game meant nothing.

"About what?"

"Not seeing into the political den of iniquity in the U.S."

Judy moved one chip to his inner board nineteen slot; she was out for blood.

"What did you observe?"

"Well, I was living in Chicago, North Side, and my Uncle Argi came to town and called me from the Drake Hotel where he was staying and invited me for dinner."

Paul rolled a five and a six; he nailed Judy at his six slot and had a scout out as well, not far, but out.

They ordered two more *ouzos* and a round of snacks. The *caffenion* was old style: high ceilings; a balcony floor over the back half; metal leg marble top tables; wooden rattan chairs half full of desultory customers sitting in twos and threes, most smoking, some playing cards, half with coffee and the others with *ouzo*; ancient filigree light fixtures hung from the ceiling but from such a height as to give enough dingy light to play or talk. Nothing was special about this *caffenion*; its type could be found throughout Greece, larger or smaller depending on the place.

"I didn't tell him that I had a long paper due the next day, which I should have done, but agreed to meet him downtown at his hotel at eight that evening. I worked on the paper longer than I should have to be on time with him, so then I took a hurried shower and dressed and got in the old Vauxhall and took off, going east on Foster to get on Lakeshore Drive and driving south to the Drake. It had started raining a steady drizzle."

Judy rolled a five and a four and moved one chip to the ten slot of her outer board.

Paul lit a cigarette, gave it to Judy, and lit another for himself.

"You've got to understand the special relationship I had with that car. It was a slow boat on the highway, but in town, it was a jet. Geared low for quick acceleration from a stop, and its body was narrow and about half the length of average American cars. I drove it like a motorbike."

"That wasn't a good idea, was it?" Judy asked as Paul rolled double fives and stacked four more chips on hers that were already nailed in her nineteen slot, his six.

"Never occurred to me. Things were just there, and I did them. Driving was always a gas, and I could dip and weave and dart and get around slower traffic like a bumblebee. And that night, being late, I was really jiving, passing on the right when parked cars stopped before the intersection and getting back into the moving lane before the first parked car of the next block. And then, like death and taxes, there was a stopped car about two lengths into the next block, and as I came back from passing on the right, there it was in front of me. I played the brakes and slowed down well for the conditions, but I rammed the car in front anyway. Not too hard, just hard enough to bend his bumper."

"Your throw," Judy said. "You weren't hurt?"

"No, nor the other guy, but the other driver was a cop. I had rear-ended a cop car!"

"Not a good idea," Judy declared.

"A terrible idea. Needless to say, I never made it to dinner with Uncle Argi, only to jail with five counts against me: passing on the right, speeding, rear-ending stationary vehicle, damage to city property and . . . what was the fifth?"

"Your throw again," Judy repeated as Paul was now looking off into the deep space of memory instead of at the backgammon board or her.

"Oh, yeah, unsafe driving for road conditions," he said and rolled double fives, stacking four additional chips on the five previously nailing her chip at slot nineteen.

"How did you get out of it?"

"They let you call help from jail, and I got a friend to come and bail me out. After I was out, I called Uncle Argi and explained what had happened. He said not to worry, he'd take care of it. The following Monday, Argi called and told me he had arranged everything and all I had to do was go to an office in the building opposite the courthouse where I was to be arraigned an hour before my court appearance time and ask for a Mr. Smith."

"Riveting name," Judy said as she rolled another five and four and covered her outlier piece; she had much better board position than him.

"Anyway, Mr. Smith came out after a bit, and he really looked the part of a politician's stooge. He was wearing a suit made from one of those shiny silver with black and gray swatches and a broad pink tie. He was not tall, but well built, and he commanded the space about him. Then we crossed to the courthouse and entered the courtroom. It was full, people everywhere, everybody waiting to be arraigned. I was following, of course, and Mr. Smith walked right up to the gate where the public area ends and waited until the judge had settled the case then pending. But as soon as that was done, and even though the clerk had called the next case, Mr. Smith approached the judge and whispered into his ear, and the judge looked at the file and called out, 'Case number A3303 dismissed, court costs only,' and banged his gavel. Mr. Smith led me out and across the hall to the cashier, paid twenty-five dollars in court costs, and wished me a good day. When I thanked him, having finally understood that the whole mess was now over and done with and I had escaped a big fine and possibly jail time, he made light of it, and when I offered to reimburse him for the court costs at least, he refused, saying, 'We take care of our own. Any time you get in trouble, give me a call,' and he gave me his card, which simply read 'Mr. Smith' and gave a telephone number."

Judy and Paul were throwing dice now to remove their pieces from the board; Judy had not trapped any of Paul's pieces in her inner board, but Paul had one of hers. Judy was idling, as she had gathered all her pieces onto her inner board except the one. Paul continued rolling the dice and moving his pieces to the initial position, from whence they could be removed. As luck would have it, he rolled double sixes for his last piece nailing hers and scooped it and three others up as the first removal. At that stage of the game, skill was replaced by the die faces that came up with each roll, and both of them were snatching pieces off the board with no clear winner evident—the end relied solely on the numbers, and they were both focused on the terminal frenzy when the backgammon board was snapped shut, almost crunching Paul's fingers.

"Stand up!" a gruff voice ordered.

"What?" they both exclaimed. They had not been paying attention to what had been happening around them in the *caffenion*, but when they looked up from their game, they saw that all the patrons were standing in a double-rank formation and were encircled by uniformed men carrying rifles.

"Get in line!" the man standing above them ordered; he was wearing the same cheap suit that Pavlos had worn.

"Who—" Paul started to say.

"Police," the suit replied.

"What—"

"Get up!"

Two uniform men approached Paul; the suit jabbed him in the shoulder.

"Get up, both of you."

Paul and Judy complied—they had no choice—and took positions at the end of the double file. Judy was the only woman in the roundup. Nothing was said, but the column started forward.

"Hands on heads, palms down!" was commanded as the communists and backgammon players were led out of the *caffenion* toward a police station. And after all the prisoners and their guards had jostled their way into it, identification papers were collected. Judy and Paul were the last to hand theirs over, British and American passports.

"Foreigners?"

"Not completely," Paul piped. "I'm also Greek, and Judy has lived here for years."

The police looked them over closely. "Why were you there?"

"We were simply drinking *ouzo,* and eating snacks, and playing backgammon," Paul explained as if innocence filled him.

The officers left the room and closed and locked the door; there were no windows. Alone with the other men caught in the sweep, they became the center of attention, especially Judy. Several of the men—there were nineteen in all—advanced toward her, but Paul stepped in front of them—not that he thought they would do her violence, but to be the "man."

No one spoke—the room would be bugged—but everyone lit a cigarette after Paul offered them from his and Judy's packs. The room was soon clouded in smoke haze, but no one objected.

The door was unlocked and opened, and a voice commanded, "Foreigners outside!"

Paul and Judy walked through the mass of the others—Judy received a number of helping hands—and their cigarette smog, and exited the holding room.

An officer handed their passports back and asked again, "Why were you there?"

"We were—" Paul began.

"Yes, yes, I know, drinking *ouzo*, eating snacks, and playing backgammon. Next time, stay in the tourist areas. Now, go home."

"Well," Judy said as they were walking back along Athena Street toward the Plaka and Anafiotika, "that wasn't much of an adventure."

"Yeah," Paul agreed, "but I think we got out just in time."

"You should go to the *caffenion* tomorrow, if it's open, and pay our bill."

When Paul met Pavlos for another lesson the next day, he asked, "What happened to those guys?

"They'll be out in two days because they were planning their demonstration for tomorrow."

"That simple?"

"Yes, it is that simple, all part of the game."

* * *

"All part of the game" caused Paul to remember a story his father had told him, although John thought of the affair in much different terms. Father and son spoke of practical matters; Paul was a good listener, and his father was an incessant source of practical advice, and a wonderful story teller, especially about Greece, but also concerning many episodes from his life in the U.S. They had little else to say to each other across the forty-two-year difference in their ages.

Paul was forever asking questions about the past. He had wanted to hear everything his father would relate from shortly after his concussion to determine if he was really the son of this couple with whom he felt vaguely related, no, probably only entwined. He hoped to find inconsistencies in the stories from before and during his early life that would prove his intuition that he was adopted. He never thought he belonged to a different family, just not to the one in which he was the dumb star and only child.

One contradiction was his father's insistence on Jane's physical and psychological distance from her mother, Maria, and his equal but opposite dedication to keeping Paul near to them. Shouldn't what was good for the younger generation be as valid for the older? Why keep his mother from her mother if he wanted Paul to stay close, very close to them? And why had his father never gone back to Greece to see his parents? But Paul knew the answer to that question, as his father always pointed out that he had eleven brothers and sisters, all of whom except for one brother in France and a sister in Joliet, had remained in Greece to care for their parents, whereas he, Paul, was the one and only.

Paul wondered if the lack of siblings was his fault?

They were walking on the other side of Central Avenue, toward the Medical Arts Building at the end of the block. Paul had volunteered to accompany his father, who had a doctor's appointment and would probably have to wait for the doctor, who had given a sliding time because he had other obligations that might run an hour to two over, but then again, might not. In exchange for a story, Paul agreed to tag along.

"Maybe I'm not supposed to see things, but I do," Paul began, as his father always gave him the choice of story setting. "It looks to me like you and Yiayia don't get along and that you don't like to visit her for long when we go to Peoria. Why?"

"Your grandmother is a good woman, and I don't want you to think otherwise. There was bad luck two times," John began. "The first I didn't know before the second. If I had—and this is why I tell you always think before you act—things might be different. We came back from honeymoon and stopped for night in Indianapolis. Since we leave Joliet on wedding trip, Jane talk about getting her hair cut now she married woman. But she afraid of what her mother say. Short hair for woman style was new. In the old thought, a woman's hair was her glory, and no good woman would cut her hair short."

"I don't understand the connection," Paul complained. "Why couldn't a good woman have short hair?"

"It comes from religion. Woman is cause of first sin and is not allowed to make herself seen and cause interest. So, long hair is natural, and short hair is risky."

Paul didn't ask for more clarification, but he felt something was wrong about risky short hair. The next day, in a book, he would come upon the word risqué, and look it up in the dictionary and think that was probably what his father had meant because it fitted the description.

"Okay," Paul said, "and then what?" At the moment, he was not enlightened but would wait for understanding.

"We talk a lot. I say do what you want with your hair. You are a legal young woman, and married now, no longer Miss, Mrs. now, and you live with me in my home, not your mother's any longer, so if you want, cut your hair. The third day of our trip in Buffalo, she have hair cut like the young fashion. All was good until Indianapolis on our return, when she lost nerve to see her mother with short hair. She was really scared. Made me mad. She wouldn't listen. We would only stay in Joliet few hours, had to get back to factory after gone ten days. She think to buy wig, but we had spent most of money, so she bought pieces that fit in her short hair and make it look long.

"Fake hair did not fool your grandmother. It looked real to me, but not Yiayia. We go up the stairs of porch, and she see us from inside and come out. She stood in front of the door and would not let us in. Instead, she scream, not even say hello, 'No daughter of mine have short hair.' Jane starts crying, and that made me mad again. Jane apologize much, but Yiayia not listen. Jane said, 'John approved.' Her mother answer, 'John not your mother, I am.' Finally, I have enough and say, 'She is your daughter, but she now my wife, and I tell her what she can do, not you, and I like short hair.' Yiayia go to pieces. Go back in house and close screen door in our face. 'Ioanna,' she said, 'you hurt me in the heart at a time like this!' But you see, we didn't know about lost checks, and Yiayia give no explanation, she just cry from other side of screen. I take your mother's arm and lead her back to car, and we drive to Peoria. Jane cry all the road. Helen call that evening and told us about lost checks and how Yiayia was so upset and how sick George become. Jane spent too much money, but she bought good wig. She would tell Yiayia that the short hair was the real wig and the long hair was hers like always. Jane and Francis, who also live in Peoria, go to Joliet in next week to see their father and for Jane to make up with her mother. But after that, Yiayia and I only friendly; she call me Mr., and I call her Mrs."

"You can go in to the doctor now," the receptionist said to John.

"You stay here. I not be long."

That was fine with Paul. He had a mountain of information to swallow. First, he could never have imagined his mother crying, and even more unbelievably, in front of, or because of, or both, her own mother. Somehow that seemed absurd. And she had been a grown, married woman. He sensed but could not articulate that there were many things in the adult world more game-like than anything children played. Adults were always certain they were right, and that took all the fun out of everything. His mother had been scolded, which meant all the scolding of him she did was at best second-hand. In his mind, if someone had power, they could not be under someone else's authority. That was that; he would no longer take his mother seriously, and if she detected his change of fear level and accused him of anything, he could respond that she was not perfect herself, and if cornered, he would remind her of cutting her hair short when she knew that was a sin, and a big one, in Yiayia's eyes.

Then there was the issue of fear. His mother frightened? From what little he knew of the devil, Paul thought it more likely that the fallen angel would be afraid of something rather than his mother. If the fearless, at least seemingly so, could be frightened, what was the use or meaning of fear? But not only fear, everything, or anything. "What was the use?" was Paul's constant question. He saw that other people knew the use of things and didn't have to ask, but nothing was clear to him. Everything had to be figured out, but he also saw that every time he thought up an answer for something, it would soon turn out to be wrong.

And finally, he had to understand a new feeling he had for his mother. In the first shock, it caused him to hate her more continuously, as she, an imperfect being, kept trying to make him perfect, or at least as she wanted him to be. But at a deeper, quieter level, it also caused him to respect her more because, for all of her outward fierceness, the person within could cry from personal shame; she was fallible after all, and that made mother and son members of the same mongrel species.

That was important to him. He was twelve—it had been six years since the accident—and the world had improved to cloudy from the muddy it had been. He was slow. He knew that. Even in Arkansas. His cousins could understand the deep southern accent, but he couldn't. When rednecks spoke, the words came out long and slow, but he couldn't interpret them and then put them together fast enough into a meaning. He often answered, sometimes yes or no, without fully understanding what had been said to him.

Paul desperately wanted to grow up. He was getting smarter, and he hoped to be about normal in another six years. He had to work harder on himself, make himself more real in the world, have a mass that could not just be pushed aside or stepped over or ignored altogether.

The next time Jane tried to spank him, he caught her hand and held it and said, "I won't let you hit me anymore." He was as tall as his mother and stronger, and he held her arm while guarding with his vision against her left hand, which was equally capable of striking a blow, until he felt her relax, and then he released her. She looked at him, and Paul thought she expressed hurt—not his, hers. Then she turned and walked away, but she said over her shoulder, "What you did was not right."

That was another thing about adults: they never explained themselves. What wasn't right?

Fortunately, the following year, he went off to school in Oklahoma, and then it was three years to finish high school in Alabama and then four years at university in Illinois, and after that, he no longer expected explanations.

* * *

"I can't get into the kitchen," Judy complained.

"I know. I'm sorry. It's terrible. He's such a mess. I'll do all the chores," Little Ann offered, hoping to mollify Judy. She and Little Ron had not yet paid rent even though they had received the first payments for the bust of Teddy, John P.'s boyfriend, who Little Ron was modeling in the kitchen of their shared, small house, through which were also entrances to the bathroom and back porch.

Paul and Judy had moved from her cracker box to a real house, and they were sharing it with Ron and Ann, prefix nicknamed the Littles.

Paul was excited to help and watch and learn from Little Ron the techniques of modeling in clay, followed by mold making and plaster casting of the finished bust.

But Paul was equally intrigued by another aspect of the event.

The Greeks of Anafiotika accepted the foreigners wholeheartedly even though they could not approve of their loose lifestyles, but that caused no dissension.

The bust of Teddy did.

Everyone had an opinion, often more than one, but all were in conflict. The distillate, however, was that the Greeks believed busts were made of great men and ancient gods. None of the foreigners had a problem with the mundanity of Teddy as a subject, and only Paul began to understand the squabble that was developing, especially as *Κυρία Σόφια*, the usual peacemaker, was firmly on the side, actually at the head, of the protesters. It was one thing for John P., the English queer, to pay for sex with poor Greek boys —at least their families fared better on the wages of sin—but it was quite another for one of these lads to be immortalized in sculpture. It was a disgrace of a noble art. It was a waste of material but also talent, as Little Ron's work displayed. It was an insult not only to the Greek sculptors, past and present, but also to the state of worth that an individual had to attain to be reproduced in clay, even more meritorious in plaster, and god forbid personal requirements to be imaged in marble or bronze.

Judy was Little Ron's public defender. The Greeks were impressed by her command of their difficult language and listened to her closely. She explained that Little Ron was a devotee of Greek art and that he was doing the bust out of economic necessity, not choice.

Everyone understood necessity.

* * *

Paul did not receive a reply until Jane arrived, bringing him, among other things, a packet from Emerald containing a letter and many photographs from her wedding.

But the totally unexpected arrival of his mother shocked Paul so forcibly that he put Emerald's communication aside and did not look at it immediately. He had felt betrayed; no one's mother just appeared unannounced and certainly unanticipated. It was inexcusable that she should come without warning him. That was not entirely true; he had received a telegram on the ninth of the month from his father stating that Jane and Mary would be staying at the Titania Hotel from the tenth.

The reason for Jane's trip was obviously an attempt to save him from himself, as both she and his father had so frequently tried to do in the past, but this was different. Now he was a man, not a boy, not in their charge, not depending upon them financially, and certainly not interested in hearing the same litany of human reasons and God-given commands on how he should live and behave.

It was a mellow evening of June holding on to the lengthening sunlight hours. The foreigners of Anafiotika—except John P., who didn't like females, not these bitches anyway—for the rest of the day, at least—company—were gathered at the *taverna*, as was their wont. Directed by *Κυρία Σόφια*, the telegraph delivery boy found the addressee there. Paul was nonplussed by the fact that he'd received a telegram at all, and his thoughts ran through the list of dreaded events. He tuned out everything: conversation, music, singing, food, wine, women—everything. His hands trembled, and Judy noticed.

"What's wrong, Paul?" she asked.

"I'm about to find out," Paul replied, fanning his face with the envelope as the warm night suddenly became horribly hot. "But whatever it is, it can't be good."

"Quiet everyone!" Judy commanded. "Paul just got some bad news."

"Yea," Little Ron interjected, "it's about time somebody else got some."

Several "Shhs" were heard as the friends turned their attention to Paul.

He unfolded the covering flap and removed the message paper from within. It was folded. He hesitated before reading it.

Judy saw his reluctance and asked, "Do you want me to read it to you?"

"No," he answered. "I think it's better that I read it rather than hear it."

He debated with himself on the length of time he should delay in learning the onerous news. Like the old man at the airport advising him that he could stuff a lifetime into a year, how many more moments could he go on living in his blissful Anafiotikan irresponsibility?

Who had died? No one, so far as he knew, was on the short list. Had the DeSoto burned? But it was a highly fireproof building with a fire-alarm system installed by the Department of Defense when the hotels in Hot Springs had been commandeered to provide recovery accommodations for wounded WWII soldiers. There was nothing explainable, then, so there must have been an accident.

Finally, Paul flattened the sheet: "Mother & M. Pappas arrive Piraeus. Stop. Stay Titania Hotel June 10. Stop Love Dad. End."

"Oh, God!" Paul exclaimed. "My mother's arriving tomorrow!"

"Paul, that's terrible," Judy said. Paul had described his mother sufficiently to foment the conclusion that Jane was on a mission of saving Paul from her. "What can you do?"

"Sink the boat and all the fools on it," Paul answered savagely.

"No," he added, correcting himself, "nothing; there's nothing to do but to see her and listen to the lecture and then walk away and join the Greek army."

"That's drastic, don't you think, Paul? You could go on as you, or we, are and put up with her interference as a minor inconvenience."

"Minor!" Paul guffawed.

"That depends on you. Are you still her little boy?" Judy asked provocatively.

Paul remained silent; he wanted to think.

Others in the party offered advice freely.

Some remarked on the Southern European straitjacket of family bonds. Still others objected, saying familial closeness and support were not all bad; they wished they'd had more in their homes as they were growing up.

Paul decided. "You're right, Judy. Life goes on despite minor inconveniences."

* * *

"My dear Paul," Emerald's letter began. He had seen his mother, received Emerald's packet and a paper-thin linen short-sleeved shirt with chocolate-colored patches on light cream background his mother had purchased as a gift for him from Tunis. He had found Hakim and explained the situation, and they had shared a joint to find the way. He was calm as he continued reading.

> Please be easy about me, I'm fine. What you have heard about my adventures is only the outside of the story. I knew years ago that Dad was developing an unnatural attraction to me as I began to fill out. You must have noticed that when the other girls my same age began maturing, they started coming to the church parties in lipstick and high heels. I continued dress-

ing as a throwback with bobby socks and pigtails, making myself as juvenile as possible. Mother was aware, the poor dear, of Dad's fixation, and it stressed her terribly. The woman—and I would say this even if I were not her daughter but was still privy to the information—is a saint. She looks so insignificant. She is not. I don't think that many women could have married, had a child by, and lived and maintained a family with a tyrant like my father. He is not a bad man; rather, he is like a rambunctious goat among docile sheep.

An aside: I was struck by your description of Aliki to Jimmy as having become even uglier than she was—I've never met the woman, so this is based on your judgment—thus heightening the contrast with her beauty as a young woman. I can vouch for the process; my mother was beautiful also. Now look at her. You didn't list the features of Aliki's ugliness, and so, I cannot compare, but with Mother, it was a reshaping of her head. Don't ask me how. They say the cranium is in its final shape and size by one's early twenties. My mother is the exception to the rule. In her youth, she had a very normal ratio between width and height of her head; you know how she looks now: her head—to be kind—is like an egg lying on its side. It was as if the weight of supporting my father's character squashed her skull. You will say that cannot happen, and so I've included a current photo and one of her younger self so you can see for yourself.

Where are the phrenologists when you need them?

Mother protected me like a lioness. When I was a child, if Dad was in a bad mood, he often tried to take it out on me. He had wanted a son, but he got an only-child daughter. She, however, always stood in his way and without regard to the threats of physical violence he made—give the guy a break; he only threatened, never acted. To make our lives bearable, both for Mother and me, I played the late—very late—bloomer. But by the time I was sixteen, that ploy began failing as my breasts grew beyond any restraint like a bra or breast-band, and my only alternative was to wear an iron lung all day.

The problem with Dad worsened. Mother had to keep repeating, "George, she's your daughter!" Over the next year and a half, the situation continued to deteriorate. It must have been soon after Jimmy heard Dad's comment that he came to me and said, 'I take you Greece. Find good husband—one no bother you."

I answered that I didn't want to get married but rather intended to go to university on the IBM scholarship. He said, "You go, but marry too."

To shorten a long story, suffice it to say that everything was arranged. I would marry Stavros, who promised not to lay a hand on me—he kissed me on the forehead at the end of the service—and to protect me so I could concentrate on my studies. Stavros is a good man. He looks out for me wonderfully, and he sees me as his daughter; he had one who died young. And the property that would have been her inheritance, a beautiful neoclassical home surrounded by gardens on all four sides of a large, tree-studded lot in the center of Athens, he has entitled to me.

Dad has quieted down. Mother is relieved of a crushing situation.

I am not ready for sex—not yet. I really want to think of nothing but mathematics, with no distractions however sweet they might be.

It turns out that Stavros is Dad's last living first cousin and Dad had wanted to bring him to the U.S. for a long time. Our marriage secured a six-month temporary but renewable visa for Stavros and, after two years, permanent residency. I hope to be starting a master's about then, and if so, I will be moving to Holland to study with a leader in my field of special interest.

The marriage—once Stavros is secure—will be annulled on grounds of no physical contact and wiped off the books.

To that end, back to the wedding night. Stavros had a chicken for the sheets. He slaughtered it in the room! It was ghastly! He had taped its peak shut so that it couldn't squawk and its legs together so it couldn't move. At the appropriate time, Stavros spread the sheets from the railing on the balcony in keeping with local traditions, and everyone was satisfied and happy that the marriage had been consummated, however unconvinced they also might have been. Still, chicken blood is the next best thing to a virgin's.

And the villagers! They are wonderful people. Such love and generosity and hospitality. If only the world were as advanced in its thoughts and feelings as the poor, backward peasants of an island mountain village, humanity would be far more advanced than it is under the yoke of what passes for advanced and enlightened perspectives.

I am with you; let's go forward to the best of the past. Why do we live history if not to learn from it?

I hope to prove mathematically that cooperation is more productive and less destructive than competition; the premise is an offshoot of game theory.

But you, my friend, are reading this after receiving it from your mother's hand. I had no idea that you were not informed that she and Mary were coming to save you. Not Mary; she's going to build a house and spend her last years on Zakynthos. They were much together before they left, and my mother was often with them. I had an ongoing report on the state of your mother's angst. Apparently, your father could no longer withstand her almost hysteric fixation on your situation and suggested that she travel with Mary to Greece and work her ideas out on you instead of on him.

"Thanks, Dad," Paul said aloud.

Whatever you do, dear Paul, please don't act hastily. Life is long, and most decisions are irrevocable and irreversible. Be calm, be open, listen to anything worthwhile others have to say, and then make your own way. You know all that; it's not for me to tell you. But sometimes, for all of us, our emotions get out of hand, and we—as the expression goes—throw the baby out with the bathwater.

Steer your life; take growth as its direction. Paul, the only thing you have to do is to work harder than you can. Stretch yourself, and take a long time experimenting with life.

I loved your tale about Anafiotika. Please write as much as possible.

Yours, Emerald.

* * *

Paul put Emerald's letter down, took another sip of coffee, and lit another cigarette as he continued sitting on the bench beneath the great tree. The female advice, then, Paul concluded—Judy and Emerald's at least—on dealing with the female (well, can mothers be seen as females by their sons?) was to remain calm and be reasonable.

The male in him kept going back, even if too late, to his initial inclination: sink the ship—blast the goddamned barge out of the freaking ocean!

Calm! Reasonable! How could he reason with a maniac?

No, that wasn't fair. His mother was really goofy only with regard to him. Music was her other passion; still, she had a dear voice but a silver ear.

He had gone to the Titania Hotel in the late morning just in time to enter the dining room before it closed for continental breakfast. If he could, he would sneak treats out for Judy.

When Jane saw him, she stood up quickly, almost upsetting the table where she had sat, rushed to him, and engulfed him in her embrace.

All the while, Paul was attempting to hold he at arm's length for the handshake he thought sufficient contact for a mother-son reunion after nine months of separation but both still on the same planet.

She patted his hair, rubbed his shoulders, looked over hers at Mary, and exclaimed, "He's so thin. I have to be careful not to squeeze him to death."

Finally, Paul broke loose from Jane's bear hug and made the gesture that he felt compelled to greet Mary after at least ten minutes of Jane-fuss, and also, if he didn't break free soon, the staff would have cleared out the food trays.

Paul, with a plate mounded with bacon, eggs over-easy, poached, and scrambled, sausages, butter croissants, yogurt, fruit, etc. that was placed in front of Jane but within easy reach of his long arm, said between mouthfuls, "You should have told me you were coming. Judy and I were preparing to leave for a four-day trip."

"I told her so," Mary offered.

"Oh, but I wanted to surprise you."

Mary read Paul's expression; it asked, 'Who is this woman?'

To surprise me! Paul wondered.

His mother and surprise did not fit in the same reality; she was relentless in her goal to guide him down the right—her—path, on which there were no storms but only smooth sailing and many grandchildren.

Paul drew on what he knew; Jane was not quite fifty; surely dementia didn't start that young, but everything about her behavior during this tête-à-tête seemed excessive in a person usually in command of themselves.

When Jane's excitement wore down, and after three cups of coffee, she needed to pee, and rather than use the common toilet off the restaurant that might not be clean and who knew what sort of people used it, she ascended to the room she shared with Mary, urging them to come up in twenty minutes.

"Do you understand?" Mary asked.

"Not completely. I've never seen her so—mellow?'

"No, it's entirely different. I've known Jane since she was a young girl, but even so, it took me time to sort it out, but we had so much of it on the ship, and we were together most of it. This change came on slowly. The greater the distance away from John, and the longer their separation, the more indecisive she becomes."

"I've seen that too, but never this obvious."

"Away from your father, she gradually loses her confidence."

"Like he's the dynamo and she's the light bulb."

"Exactly!" Mary concurred "She seems to be the power source when, in fact, he is."

* * *

Paul and Jane made arrangements to meet the next day, just the two of them, for lunch, Paul's treat; he wanted to show his mother that he was not one step above skid row. He was simply frugal—

had to be, and yes, Judy had enjoyed the treats he'd brought her from the breakfast bar yesterday.

Upon their meeting, Paul was determined to punish his mother with his command of Greek; he spoke it better than she even though it was her mother tongue, but she had not used it extensively except at home and always on the same narrow range of subjects. They ordered, ate, chatted, and drank coffee, Paul smoked, and they laughed at shared memories, as their sense of comedy did narrowly overlap. Paul was relaxing; his mother could be not half so bad as he envisioned at times, he allowed. Jane too was calm and happy.

"Am I to meet Judy?" she asked.

"You want to?" he shot back, amazed.

"Well, of course. If you like her, won't I?"

"Ah," Paul said, stalling. "I think that our criteria for liking someone are different." Paul wouldn't add that he dug Judy most when he was shagging her.

"Well, let's see."

"O-kay," Paul allowed slowly. "I'll mention it to Judy and see when she has free time. Her schedule of lessons is pretty tight. She's gotten as much as forty-five Drachmas per hour."

"That's good pay, is it?" Jane inquired. "A dollar and a half an hour?"

"I'll say," Paul responded, not catching his mother's tone. "One hour brings in more than our rent for the month. The most I can get is twenty, partly due to accent but also to the fact that I'm not as good as Judy; word gets around."

"She sounds very interesting, Paul. Do you love her?"

Klaxons blared in Paul's spinning brain. His mother was actually asking him serious questions instead of telling him the answers; unprecedented.

The question was also almost unanswerable. "Y-e-a-h," Paul began tentatively. "Well, I mean—" he said, trying to evade. "The thing is—" he clarified.

"But you love her enough to live with her, don't you?"

"Yes," Paul admitted, dipping his head and looking away from his mother's searching eyes.

"Then, I'd say you love her, and if you love her enough to live with her, surely you love her enough to marry."

"Marry!" Paul blurted out, reverting to English.

He was spooked. This was not his mother. Some alien being had taken residence in her form, but it wasn't her.

"I am certain Judy would prefer to be married. Most women would."

The "A-h" was drawn out; the "m-a-y-b-e" even more so. "I've never thought about it. Judy hasn't either."

"You two have not discussed the prospect at all?" Jane asked, her spirits one negative answer away from soaring.

"No, never. In fact, the opposite. We've both affirmed that we don't want to get married—I don't mean to each other. I mean at all."

"That's good," Jane adjudged.

"Why?"

"It means neither of you have ulterior motives."

If Paul hadn't been stunned like an octopus knocked senseless by dynamite fishing, he would have seen through the rehearsed line; he would have staked his life that his mother never used catch phrases ordinarily.

"What kind of motives, then?" Paul asked to gain time and rearrange his mind.

"Real motives like respect and esteem and affection."

Instead of gaining time, Paul was losing it.

He now had a mission. He would find Judy and tell her Jane's suggestion.

"Shall we?" Paul asked his mother. They had finished their last coffee. "I'll walk you back to the hotel."

"No, dear, don't bother," Jane said, absolving him. "I want to dilly-dally with shopping going back."

* * *

"Judy!" Paul shouted; he'd awakened from his after-lunch nap as she'd entered their place. "You can't imagine what my mother said."

"Oh, yes I can. How many times did she call me a gold-digging slut?"

"No, no, you've got it all wrong; she said we should marry."

"What?" exploded from Judy's mouth like a torpedo being launched.

"Yeah, I know, but she said that if we love each other enough to live together—that's the hard part, not just seeing each other, but the daily grind—then we probably love each other enough to marry."

"I'm in shock," Judy declared and sat down on the bed beside Paul. "Marriage? That's ridiculous. Marriage is garbage unless you're raising a family, and I'm a long time off from wanting to have children."

"She said—I'll give you her arguments—that women in general want to be married to a good man; naturally, she thinks I am one. She said that in the modern world, a single woman is in a precarious situation, that being married adds to a woman's stature —"

"I'm as tall as I want to be, thank you," Judy interrupted.

"That marriage brings added attention to the partner."

"More like forces."

"That a recognized legal union can become a personal partnership in which each of the pair amplifies the good qualities of the other."

"Or the worst."

"Yeah, I've never figured that out. My parents argue all the time—I mean, all the time; call it continuous—maybe not when they're asleep, but all the waking hours. It gives me a stomachache to listen to them go on and on and on, but it just seems to rev them up. It's like arguing is their hobby—other couples have golf or hiking or flower arranging; they argue. If I had been either one of them, I would have divorced the other long ago, but I've only seen one crack in their relationship, and when the external misunderstanding was explained, they were back to normal, i.e., at each other's throat, but warmly."

"What was the cause?"

"Well, a letter arrived about a month before we three were to sail in '56 on the *Olympia* from New York to Piraeus from a man who said he thought he was Dad's bastard son. He said he didn't write to ask for anything, he only wanted to know who his father was and that he had investigated the matter as much as he could and my dad was the most likely candidate. Dad showed the letter to Mother, obviously not thinking anything of it. Let me tell you, her Greek went into high gear as she read it, and the temperature began dropping immediately. I mean immediately. I could feel it. Rage? Disdain? She didn't give Dad the innocent until proven guilty bit; he was guilty that moment, and she made it clear that except for absolutely unavoidable emergencies, she was not speaking to Dad until the mess was cleared up."

"As a young man, you said your father had been a sailor."

"Right, first the navy in World War One and then a merchant marine."

"So, he could easily have fathered a child he knew nothing about. Sailors especially: here today, gone tomorrow, but leaving a seed behind."

"Right on, the very problem."

"I don't see it."

"Mother went berserk! No, I mean the other way, frozen, Arctic, Antarctic, no, the moon. A full moon in cold white, she was like that. You couldn't ignore her presence, but you couldn't get her attention. A block of ice. And the change happened like that, while she was reading the letter."

"You are not telling me why she reacted so violently."

"I don't know. Rage? Jealousy? Disdain for him because he had not married her as a virgin as she married him? I don't know; you tell me."

"That doesn't make sense."

"As if my mother should make sense."

"How old was your father when they married?"

"Forty."

"And she?"

"Twenty-five."

"Not a sheltered, foolishly romantic schoolgirl, a woman. No reasonable person would expect a forty-year old man marrying for the first time—it was his first, right—to be a virgin, especially not one who had been a sailor," Judy said, summing up the situation.

"Unless you're Jane."

"So, how did it turn out?"

"Like I said, permanent dry-ice frost for the month before sailing, and not even ten days of sun deck lounging warmed her a degree. Mind you, I didn't mind, because she got off my back as well. She didn't just put Dad on her shit list; she put me on it too, maybe males in general. But it was great; she ignored me for the first time in my life. Not feeling her eyes staring down on the top of my head and the back of my neck was the sensation of being free at last. But good things always end. Dad wanted to settle the affair; he had reached his limit of her silent bitchiness, and so, the second day we were in Greece, we all went to the man's address— sort of like people getting ready for a duel. The man was also a baker, as my dad had been, and he had a very small bakery in one of the poorest neighborhoods of Piraeus. We entered. He was in the back, but the door jingle jangled, and he came out. Asked how he could help us. Dad held out the letter and asked if he had sent it. The man looked at the letter, looked at Dad, and both of them started laughing heartily. There was zero possibility of father-son, but separated fraternal twins, they might have been. And I swear that just as quickly as Mother had turned frigid, she melted, and I felt that change too."

"See, that's the crap that fills a marriage."

"Yeah," Paul agreed, shaking his head, feeling again the weight of the contention that had been invigorating them but enervating him since the accident.

"Notwithstanding the fact that either your estimation of her, with which you've formed my impression, must be terribly wrong, or there's a game being played here that you don't see."

"I do know, and Mary confirmed it; when she's away from Dad, she loses confidence and softens her demeanor. But the question is, do you want to meet her? I didn't oblige you in any way. I said if you have time, you'd probably come, but it was unlikely you would be able to."

"That was a flimsy feint."

"Whatever," Paul responded, "but it's on you. If you decide not to come, I'll invent a reasonable excuse."

"Will the friend of hers come too?"

"Mary? Why not? She'd be a buffer."

"All right, arrange it. Since we planned to travel this weekend, I have tomorrow and the day after free. And it should be interesting to see how well you know your mother, who suggested you marry me. Unbelievable," Judy stated.

5: CHARACTERS:

EFRAT, THE FILLED

"I knew what that bastard was after, and I want it too, but not his way. God, I hate that type," Efrat said. She darted her head backwards and with a quick side-to-side toss of long tufts of tightly curled and uncommonly dense russet-colored hair.

She was a Jewess with obvious Levantine characteristics, brown skin, heavy eyebrows, and, in general, except for her prominent and hawkish nose, pretty, as experienced women often are.

"Paul, good thing you forced him to return those books—"

"You mean Leslie?" Paul asked, surprised that Efrat would stoop so low to the cradle.

"The same shithead. He's been hanging around me and pestering me continuously. I mean, I've gotten bunches of stuff outta him, and maybe ten meals and lots of drinks. But he's such a slushy type, trying to psyche me into having sex with him. If he'd just said, 'Hey, I want to fuck,' his prick would be broken by now. But when a guy comes at me as if getting sex is his reward for my loss, I want to cut his balls off, and that's the way Leslie is."

"Damnedest thing," Paul observed, "his father, Leslie Senior—so, you're talking about Junior—is a really great guy. Imagine, he actually thanked me for threatening to beat up his son, said that he had been so ashamed when he'd learned about the book thefts that he'd wanted to knock Junior around himself, but couldn't because of his wife."

"Yeah, well then, Junior, we'll call him, said his father's in Greece for a year on sabbatical from Columbia working on Byzantine-era poets who are largely unknown and overlooked but great writers. That's according to him," Efrat stated.

The other members of Leslie Wilder Senior's family—wife and two daughters—had been happy to experience a year of life in Europe; Junior, however, had thrown a fit. He hadn't wanted to miss his final year at high school with all his buddies to go anywhere, certainly not to Greece. Junior refused to go to school or take Greek lessons or become interested in anything; he was in a long sulk. When he was not stealing books, he spent most of his time trying to pick up women at the beach, and he wasted money —his and every cent he could get, beg, or steal—by his own admission.

Junior had stopped coming to the foreign Anafiotikans' evening meal at the *taverna* after the fracas with Paul. That was both a psychological relief for the regulars, as no one liked his juvenility, and an economic burden on them, as they had allowed Leslie access to their company only if he paid the entire bill; otherwise, in his absence, they divided it up equally between themselves. The kid was fifty-two years younger than the oldest of them, Jason, and his immaturity was taxing. Paul, one of the youngest regulars, was only four years older than Leslie Junior; still, the difference in their comportment was disproportional to their ages.

"I don't get it, Efrat. You're a full-bore woman. What do you see in a runt like Junior?"

"Well, I had a dry spell in finding, as you put it, full-bore men, so I decided to play with the boy. First because he had been pestering me to deflower him even though I reminded him that I was only a few years younger than his mother, and second because I felt like being mean."

"And were you?" Judy asked.

"Unmercifully," Efrat hissed. Then she continued, saying, "At some moment, or many, all women get a mirror and look at their twats, wouldn't you agree, Judy?"

"Usually quite young, I would say," Judy responded.

"Right. Well, since the last time I had looked at mine, a juxtaposition had popped into my mind. So, I got both the old camera and the twat out and took close-up photographs of the mouth of my vagina with the labia peeled back but real close up on black and white film. I showed Junior two of them, one a little closer, with the stretched-out cunt opening completely filling the frame—very abstract—and the other from further back that also showed the pee hole. And I told him that I would fulfill his request and fuck his balls off if he could name the animal in the photo. For clues, I told him it had multiple appendages, was smart and sly, and tasty and chewy and satisfying to eat. He couldn't name it, so I gave him another clue but, this time, a misleading one; I told him to go down to the fish market and have a look at invertebrates with multiple appendages and a reputation for being smart and sly.

"He came back very proud of himself and certain that he was going to get laid and said, 'I know the animal. The photo is of an octopus's mouth.'

"But if it's its mouth, where's its beak?"

"'Huh,' he said, reverting to a typical teenage reply.

"I told him it didn't matter, that he had been a good student after all and that he was going to get his reward from me. He has a motorbike, and I asked him to take us to a beautiful beach that I know where nobody goes because it is strewn with small but mostly smooth pebbles instead of sand. The soles of my feet are hard, and walking on a bumpy surface is no problem for me, but for him, stepping on rocks was like walking on embers. He 'ouched' and cursed and whined. The beach is very wide, and by the time he got to the shoreline, I had already had my swim and had prepared my surprise."

"And that was?" Paul asked, intrigued.

Jason was telling Phyllis another fantastic tale from his soldier-of-fortune life at one end of the table and had the men's (Big and Little Ron and Nick) attention, while Efrat held the women's (Cleopatra, Little Ann, and Judy) and Paul's at the other. They were gathered at their table in the *taverna,* but since Leslie Junior was absent, their meal was the simple menu: salads, appetizers, and carafes of house wine and *tsipouro.*

"Why, of course, I filled my cunt with smooth, almost polished, rounded pebbles."

"You did what?" Little Ann asked incredulously.

83

"Don't you occasionally?" Efrat asked, seemingly surprised. "It's great fun and a form of mechanical douche and good exercise for the pussy muscles. And it's sexy fun as well, 'cause the pebbles hit all the right spots. You walk and swim, holding them in, and then you get on land and expel them one by one like you were spitting at a spittoon," Efrat explained.

"Well, I never heard of such a thing," Little Ann pontificated. "We don't do that kind of crazy stuff in Australia."

"Well, in Israel, many of the Jewish girls do," Efrat added, and her expression was becoming ever more sly. "We learn the trick during military service."

"You were in the army?" Cleopatra asked, wondering how the women kept their nails from breaking doing army-type things.

"Universal conscription for both men and women, all, that is, except for the ultra-orthodox who pray and study and perform rituals all day."

"But why?" Judy asked.

"Oh, they're very devout."

"No, I don't mean that," Judy protested. "I mean the other, the pebbles."

"Why, of course, to fuck him up as he was trying to screw me. Don't you see, there was no room at the inn," Efrat said, and she smiled broadly at her turn of phrase. "He was like the Big Bad Wolf; he huffed, and he puffed, but he couldn't get in. Then I started bucking on him, and he was crying out, 'Ouch, that hurts!' I pushed him off me and got up and went back into the sea and said, 'I'm going to stay here and swim for a while, and then, when I'm ready, I'll hitchhike back. You go on home now to your momma. You're not ready for a woman yet.'"

"Oh, shit!" Paul interjected. "The poor bastard is probably ruined for life."

"Tough," Efrat declared. "Anybody who steals books from libraries gets no sympathy from me."

On that point, all agreed.

JASON, THE CAPTAIN

Of the foreign contingent of Anafiotikans, Efrat and Jason stood out, Efrat because she said whatever occurred to her and had set herself the goal of photographing every person in the world—well, at least, everyone who lived in the Plaka—and Jason because he had a young mind in an old and bruised and misused body.

"Once I used a fishing trawler to run guns," Jason was relating now for everyone's attention. "We had purchased our merchandise in Cape Town, sailed around the Cape of Good Hope, and we were drawing abreast of Cape Agulhas when it happened."

Jason had all of his audience's attention, and so he fell silent to lengthen the anticipation. He stroked his full white beard —Hemingway trim—and patted his hair, also full and white. The surface of his facial skin was smooth between the two diagonal scars that marked his left check.

"And?" Phyllis coaxed.

"Joha," Jason continued, "my cabin boy, ran into the wheel house. I have seen great fear in men's eyes but never so much as blared out of his. 'Cap! Cap!' he screamed, but he could say nothing more; rather, he was looking toward the stern and pointing.

"But first, I said we were off the Cape of Agulhas, which doesn't mean anything unless you know that is where the Southern Atlantic mixes with the western extent of the Indian Ocean. Close to shore, the waters are shallow and treacherous, so larger ships sail beyond the continental shelf. Because the two oceans' currents mix from opposite directions with different velocities and with different temperatures, high seas are frequent, but monster waves are not, but when they do occur, deadly. But that's not right, because nobody really knows what causes them. Just theories for landlubbers. Very few sailors who have encountered them live to relate the experience, and I am one of them.

"The sea was running high, choppy like angrily boiling water, and the wind was strong but not gale force. The helmsman had the wheel while I was looking at charts and plotting our course. I ran to the side of the wheelhouse where Joha was pointing and looked back across the stern, but I couldn't see anything unexpected at first glance. My man finally managed to speak, and he said, 'Sea done drunk de sun!'

"'Joha, it's only sunset,' I said to reassure him, but I had a sinking feeling because Joha knew the seas and skies much better than I, and he wouldn't have been so frightened if he had not seen something ominous.

"The ship's prow was rising on a crest as the stern was falling into the trailing trough. That put the horizon behind higher than ahead. All normal except that as the stern rose, riding over the crest of the next wave, the horizon behind didn't drop but continued rising. 'We done for! De comin!' Joha shouted. Then I saw it, a monstrously high wall of water—and it was like a wall, vertical. Surfers ride the bottom of the wall as big waves are breaking, but the one coming up on us wasn't breaking. The hatches had been battened down before we left port, but I knew that when the wave hit, the hatches would give way, maybe even the deck. There was nothing to do; we were doomed. I thought for a moment of trying to turn the ship into the wave that was rearing up from behind, but there was no time, and even if I had, it would have made no difference. Joha had been on deck and was wearing a life jacket, and so was the helmsman, by regulation, but I wasn't. Then I had this serendipitous moment. Sound stopped, and time with it. I knew I was a dead man just waiting to die."

"Oh, Jason!" Phyllis cried.

"Not the only time, my dear, but as you can see and feel, I'm still here in the flesh."

"Jason, don't interrupt your story," Judy pleaded.

"Where was I? Yes, in that moment, that wonderful moment when you know your fate, your very existence is out of your influence—I won't say control, no one is in control of their fate even if they think they are. And you know that whatever living you're going to do, you'd better hurry and do it as the last minutes, if you are lucky, seconds if not count down. I didn't see my life flash before my inner eye like so many survivors of near death describe; rather, I saw the scenes of all the death and destruction I had caused in my life as a montage. Then I saw that the man who had done these horrible deeds was called Jason but was, in fact, the invention of his environment. A mouse without reference to its scale can think it is a huge bear.

"Do you see what I mean?

"I mean that any creature is some small part of its personal nature, but it is, in main, a creation of its surroundings—location, location—and family condition and a thousand influences that are different for each person or being, yet common to all."

Jason had been a soldier of fortune and a mercenary in his youth, but he was their elder, their captain, their silver-back. None of the men, least of all Paul, not even Big Ron, the mostly likely contender, wanted to challenge him. And the women, they all loved and allowed him, invited even, to flirt with them.

None of the friends objected to his statement, and they all waited for clarification.

"My fear of death vanished because, and this is strange, it had arrived; death was here and now and was no longer coming. I felt free, and for the first time, I, Jason the person, not Jason the product of a particular set of circumstances and situations, knew that I was like an ant in a larger perspective than I ordinarily viewed, but an ant that at the last moment, looked up and saw the forest towering over it while still being at home within it."

"How did you escape the wave?" Judy asked; she was less interested in Jason's philosophical musing and more in the action of his story.

"I didn't," Jason answered. "I gave myself to serenity. I was anticipating what life after death, if it exists, was like.

"The wave didn't break on the ship; instead, it simply rolled over us like a vacuum cleaner. One second normal—well, as normal as a stormy ocean can be—and next, water everywhere outside, and the next—we had light in the wheelhouse, the engine was still running—we, the ship, was rolled, not port to starboard, but stem to stern." Jason demonstrated with his spoon.

"Oh, Jason, that must have been terrible," Phyllis lamented.

"Not a bit, my dear," Jason assured her. "The hard part about death is accepting it; after that, it is of no consequence." He looked around the table at his friends, all much younger and more impressionable than he, and showed them his expression of calm.

"And?" Judy prodded again.

"I have no idea. When I regained consciousness, I was lying belly down on the bottom of a lifeboat's hull. It was morning. The sea was calm. There was no one and nothing around me. And I got mad at fate. What the fuck was going on? I had been in a perfect place and time to die due to circumstances beyond my knowledge or ability to influence, but there I was, saved so that I would have to die all over again, and it just pissed me off. I was thirsty. That's the big problem if you survive a sinking. Then the pain started. First, my head. I reached to the side of my forehead in front of the temple, and a flap of skin fell to the corner of my eye. Then my breathing was unbearable: four broken ribs on one side and cracked on the other. I didn't know the count at the time, of course; I could only measure the pain. Now, you see, everything was changed. Death had backed off and was hiding in the shadows again. Serenity was shattered. It had been snuffed out by the desire to live, and you know, the funny thing is that under ordinary circumstances, one is not usually aware of a desire to live, because one is simple living day by day. But make the situation you're in desperate, and the will to live flames like a volcano. I couldn't move much—really, only my head and arms. I was in front of empty ocean that stretched all along the horizon, as far as I could see. But my most immediate problem was managing the pain. I knew I couldn't allow myself to fall into shock. I lay my head down on the side I thought least damaged and visualized a calming balm flowing through my brain, quenching the fire in the neurons. When I woke up again, I was in the sickbay of a South African navy destroyer."

"What time period?" Paul asked.

"Not long, forty-four hours."

"Forty-fours! It's a miracle you survived."

"No, it's not, Paul. It's statistics. Some number of people lost at sea for various reasons will be saved in different ways. I've been outside the law and common custom since I became a man because the way things were seemed fake to me. I examined everyone close to me and things in my purview and how people would argue, and violently at times, about things they could forgive or ignore had their ego not been goading them to take offense. I didn't buy into the bullshit and did what I liked. My only connection with law and authority was not getting caught; there's a lot of room between the seams, and there are a lot of seams.

"People were not persons, I saw them as if they were chess pieces in a game that never stopped, but only timed out eventually for every player, champion, novice, or dunce. When you learn to see others as objects, not necessarily for exploitation, just for clarity, or call it objectively, you understand that if one object or more survives a disaster, it's not a miracle, only a probability, just as how, if one or more objects are lost, it's not a damnation, only an eventuality."

"All right," Paul conceded, "but it's still remarkable."

"My whole life has been, my boy, my whole life."

PHYLLIS, THE FEINT

When Phyllis returned from her journey in Afghanistan, she was almost penniless. During her absence, Jason had settled in Anafiotika. Within moments of their meeting, they had made a deal: her poverty balanced his age, and she moved in with him.

Lillian was furious. Only her good breeding prevented her from voicing her wrath to everyone except Peter; even a saint needed one outlet.

"How could she stoop to live with that old lecher?" Lillian demanded.

"You've never seen him. How can you characterize the man?" Peter had asked. He couldn't just attend to Lillian in bed; he had to pretend to be interested in her complaints as long as they were directed against someone else.

"She is a bloody duchess!" Lillian exclaimed as she bowed to blue blood in the vernacular. "Has she no shame?" she asked rhetorically, knowing the answer. She had confronted Phyllis in person. and it was that exchange Phyllis now shared with the *taverna* crowd.

"Yours and mine," Phyllis replied, acknowledging Jason's claim. "Only our lives take place in different worlds that overlap only in Anafiotika.

"I was saved from a human sea that was trying to swallow me as surely as any ocean was trying to drown you. I had a fresh, and I will say unexpected, dousing today from Lillian. We had arranged to meet this morning in Kolonaki, the only square in Athens where she is comfortable."

"She said she wouldn't set foot in the Plaka, let alone here," Paul said, "We've been to her place, and it's very nice, I admit, but it's the same old shit wherever there's money; she, on the other hand, won't visit us. Anafiotika is much too filthy for her. What if she had to pee?"

"She would piss on herself," Phyllis answered. "She certainly let loose on me."

"On you?" Little Ann exclaimed, horrified at the thought that anyone would sully an aristocrat. Being a colonial, she was divided between awe and affront for the institution.

"About Jason, she said I made a bad deal living with an old lecher. That I owed it to myself, my class and country to live up to what it means to be a duchess.

"So, I asked, 'But Lillian, what does being a duchess mean?'

"She almost gagged. 'You are one. You should know.'

"'Yes,' I replied, 'I do know. It means we, British aristocratic women, compete to wear the silliest possible hat because the queen likes silly hats and she is the arbitrator of style within the court. It means that our relationships are based more on material considerations than personal predilections like the man one can love but whom one may marry only if he has the title, the influence, the money, the property, the polish, the accent, the dark skin that fades to chalk in winter gloom that peerage demands. It means a lot of things of which I am sated, and from which I ran to Greece on Judy's invitation.'

"'Well,' Lillian said, 'I am here too at Judy's . . . because of Judy.'

"I'm flattered," Judy announced. "I've never been the reason for anything before."

"No, Jud'," Big Ron interjected, "you were the one who convinced me to live in Anafiotika."

"And us too," Little Ann added. "I mean, we live in your house, and we haven't paid you any rent yet, but we will as soon as John P. gives us an advance."

"I'm not doing it!" Little Ron insisted.

"Oh, yes, you are, dear. Remember that tonight, we have to borrow from Paul to pay for our dinner. We can't do that every night, can we, dear?"

"So, you really have a title?" Cleopatra asked.

"I really have a title. Really two: the duchess business, but I was born to that, and then, by my own actions, I have earned another class of epitaphs that define me, like black sheep, fallen woman, class disgrace, ungrateful issue, and many more I will not mention other than to say they are all in the same vein."

"What crime did you commit?"

"Well, I gathered all the cash I could for a number of years and deposited it in a numbered rather than named account, and when I had amassed enough to amuse myself for a few years, I staged my death."

"So, your family thinks you're dead?"

"No, they found out. My siblings ratted me out. I had confided in no one, certainly not in them, but they—brother and sister, both younger—hired a detective. My plan was good but not perfect, and then I got careless after two years of hiding, and I was uncovered."

"Why did they get a detective and not your parents? With one child out of the way, there would have been more for them."

"Ah, so it would seem, but the English system of lineage can be very complicated. My family's duchy is entailed to the first born of every generation regardless of sex. Very forward looking for the times even if, until the recent past, a first-born female could not inherit in her own name but had to acquire her wealth through a husband. The title is singular and does not extend to the spouse, nor does it descend to younger siblings. If I die before my father, and I have not produced offspring, the title dies too unless, before he died, he were to divorce my mother, kill my brother and sister, and marry another woman who is virgin but fertile and will soon deliver another first born."

"Wow, a real Agatha Christie," Paul observed. "Okay, so the others are out of luck whatever happens, and since you're not on good terms with them, why would they want you found?"

"To avoid death duties. When my father dies, and if I were presumed dead, the estate will be gutted by death duties twice because there will have been no interval for it to recover value before the next death duty tax. On the other hand, if I am actually the fool they think I am, they believe they can persuade me to gift them what I decline, as that will be taxed at a lower rate. It is all about money. Do you not agree?" Phyllis asked, looking at each of them in turn. "On that side," she continued, "it is all about money, but on this side, it is sharing cabbage salad and tavern wine with friends who have no more money than to get barely by."

"Lady Phyllis," Little Ann began.

"Phyllis is enough."

"It seems to me that you're avoiding something most people would die for."

"Maybe, until they had it."

"Do you never plan to go back?" Cleopatra asked.

"Oh, I will go back and do a year of penitence, and then all will be forgotten, and I will be reinstated to my inheritance again, but not in the near future.'

"She means not until I die," Jason added.

"I will be an old lady by then. No one will know me."

"Nonsense, my dear. I have been ready to die for a long time now. But one lifeboat after another saves me. You came into my life completely by chance but have filled it with more air and light and sweetness than I knew in all my years before."

"I will keep you alive, you old lecher, for a long time before I have to become a duchess again."

ANN, THE LITTLE

"I never imagined that I would someday sit across a dinner table with a duchess," Little Ann said.

"Why is the royalty thing so important to you, Little Ann?" Paul inquired.

"But are you royalty, Phyllis, or only nobility?" Nick, who rarely spoke, asked.

"Nobility. But please, let us drop the subject."

Unmindful, Paul continued, saying, "So, nobility is not necessarily royalty?"

On the status of her celebrity fascination, Little Ann was unequaled. She was an avid reader of the gossipy media, newspapers and magazines, in awe of important people, not of what they had accomplished, since many celebrities didn't do much else except be themselves, but rather of the fact that they stood out from the crowd. She wanted, craved distinction, and she garnered attention, but not in ways that pleased her. She was short, almost five feet tall. Her hair looked like the setting sun had dipped behind a fuzzy cloud. With a face interesting but not pretty—too full—and a body shapely but too girthy, she was pursing her dream for recognition through Little Ron, her incestuous son-like husband, who was a mess of a man but a superb sculptor.

"To be royalty, their duchy must have been bestowed upon a member of the then monarch's family, by no means necessarily in line for the throne. The nobility includes those of rank who are not directly connected to the ruling house, and that must be Phyllis's station. And finally, the aristocracy also includes people of wealth and power who have no connection to the peerage class."

"She wastes a lot of time reading those damned rags."

"Do you suffer, dear?" Little Ann asked sarcastically. "When did you last go without a meal, or clean clothes, or a bed for your bony body and a pillow for your brilliant head? When? Do you remember? I don't."

Little Ron issued a sound like "Hum" but less thoughtful.

"Do you see how hard it is?" Little Ann asked the table at large, although Phyllis remained her focus. "I have to make something of him." She paused to tip her head in a disparaging nod toward Little Ron, but at the same time, she raised her arm to his shoulder and lightly massaged his neck. "There's nothing I can do with myself. I mean, look at me. At home, we always had food on the table but, too often, not very much for all our hungry mouths. Mother always waited to eat last; she was very thin. None of us got the nutrition we needed, and there sure wasn't any possibility of vitamin supplements, and we kids were all short and wide except Billy, who was tall and thin but died at twelve.

"How is it right—not even fair, just right—for one's future to be determined by others' pasts? Why was I not Phyllis? I would never suggest that she should have been me, only that I, or anyone, need the possibilities and the support that she had."

"But how do you know about the opportunities Phyllis may have had?" Cleopatra asked.

"Look at her! Look at you, but look at her first. Her poise, her natural command, her speech, her accent, her posture . . . do you want more?"

"And look at you! You're probably the most beautiful woman I've ever seen, but you're no taller than me. You are slimmer, and that makes you look taller, but you're not. And you wear heavy makeup wonderfully. Don't we call you Cleopatra because you are so beautiful? Liz Taylor shouldn't have gotten the role, you should have.

"And you have Nick, a beautiful scabbard for your sword. Look at my bloke; I have to help him keep his knuckles from dragging on the floor.

"I don't wear any now, but when I did, I used—like any woman—makeup as a mask, a way of getting beyond myself. And you! None of us—maybe Nick, but I doubt even he—has ever seen you without your face on. We have you close, and we love you, but none of us knows who you are as the other Little Ann. We only know Cleopatra."

ANN, THE CLEOPATRA

"I don't know what to say," Cleopatra responded.

"You don't have to say anything," Little Ron stated. "She gets this way sometimes."

"No, she's right. I do hide behind my primping. I would shoot Nick if he ever saw me without my face on, as you say, but then, I use waterproof makeup.

"My mask is really a shield. If I'm not behind it, men pester me, but when they have to deal with my sexuality exaggerated through it beyond their confidence, they leave me alone."

"Good tactics, girl," Jason allowed. "the best defense is a good offense; even George Washington agreed with you."

"No, Jason, that's male thinking. I don't want to fight at all. I want to be left in peace," Cleopatra corrected.

"I was told," she continued, "and the mirror confirms it, that my eyes are too open, too large, that my sexuality and sensuality have less sultriness because they are like beacons, flashlights almost."

RON, THE LITTLE

"No, Cleopatra," Little Ron insisted. "Sculptures and paintings that emphasize large, open eyes like yours are showing the way to the inner person. You would be a perfect model."

"Thank you, Little Ron. Do you think I have a soul? Nick doesn't."

"I have never said that," Nick protested.

"You never say much of anything," Cleopatra complained. "Certainly, you have never mentioned seeing into my soul through my eyes."

"Pardon the observation, Nick, but you rarely speak; are you quiet only among others or always?" Phyllis asked.

"Neither. When I have something to say, I speak, but talking without a purpose has never appealed to me."

"Never mind, Nick. I talk enough for both of us," Little Ron offered.

"Dear, you mean you mutter a lot, but you don't say much."

Little Ron gestured, throwing his long arms above his head. "I surrender." He laughed. "I can't win anyway. I said clearly and over and over that I didn't want to do a bust of that prick's boyfriend, but you said I had to; that's why I mutter."

"We have to pay Paul and Judy a fair share of rent. We have to eat, and we have other expenses . . . do you have another suggestion?"

95

"I would like to see your work," Jason said. "Paul tells me it's very good, very classical and—"

"That's it!" Little Ron declared, becoming animated for the first that evening other than when eating. "The Greek sculpture is so dynamic, so proportioned . . . Have you looked closely at how they did the material of their dresses? The marble seems as delicate as the cloth it depicts. Bodies are idealized, sure, but faces are suspended between realistic depiction and a visible abstraction of thought. The Romans went too far into representation; their busts are portraits of individuals, not the expression of humanity through the person, as are the Greek."

"He won't listen to me," Little Ann bemoaned. "That's what John P. wants. His Teddy as his Teddy is, not as Little—"

"I'm Ron to you, not Little Ron."

"Yes, dear, but as I was saying, John P. wants an exact rendering of Teddy's face, but my Ron insists on giving it greater depth, more universality."

RON, THE BIG

"And well he should," Big Ron said, entering the discussion for the first time. "He's making art, not a death mask."

"Thanks, Big Ron, you understand," Little Ron said.

"You are definitely welcome, Little Ron," Big Ron replied. "I have the same problem with publishers. They want characters who have depth but do not confuse the reader by being many sided, fully rounded with the shit and the sugar and a lot of mixes between. I can't see people that way, or that is, I do see people that way, in the raw, with their many sides. John P. is a base queer and should be castrated for exploiting poor young Greek boys with his English pounds, but he's also a thoughtful and sympathetic man. Can you imagine how hard that is to make real? To develop a character who is split into two at least and many more parts? Characters will always display internal contradictions naturally. I mean, we all have them. We know that about ourselves, but apparently, when reading fiction, we want our heroes and heroines to be solid. It doesn't matter how. They can be solid bad, or good, or even some of both, but not fractured between good qualities and bad, gross thoughts and deep insights, violent sex and tender feelings. But that's who we really are, not obviously because the behaviors and attitudes are expressed over time in different places with different people. But when you are writing it, all of time has to find a way into the word after word on the page."

NICK, THE SILENT

"I tried writing prose," Nick began, and everyone focused on him, not only for what he might deign to say or to hear his thoughts. Nick was a perfect specimen of the human male. His height and width were in perfect proportion: his face was symmetrical, his hair blond and in close-cut, loose curls, and his body was the miracle of constant exercise, good nutrition and habits, and youth. "And that was a problem," he said, continuing his rare speech. "You have to get, or feel you do, everything down at once. That's why I write poetry now. You sense how much can go into each line."

JUDY, THE UNREQUITED

"In drawing, you can do the same thing. I won't say painting, but drawing can get close to the essence of a thing. And a drawing doesn't have to fill the page, because the open places are as much a part as the penciled," Judy offered.

"Are you ever going to finish the drawing you started of me?"

"No, Big Ron, I'm not."

"Why?"

"I've told you."

"Because I remind you too much of him."

"Exactly."

"Why didn't you see that before you started?"

"Maybe I did. Maybe that's why I wanted to draw you, but then we started sleeping together, and that overloaded my circuits."

"So, you dumped me—."

"Don't be dramatic. You weren't in love with me; you just wanted a handy screw."

"That's not fair. And what about that guy on the island? You traded both of us in for Paul?"

"You had a thing with Big Ron?" Paul asked Judy; he knew about Φούσκις, but this was the first he'd heard about Big Ron, not that it mattered.

"Well, we didn't live together like you and I do now," she answered.

"Sorry, Paul, but you don't look at all English," Big Ron observed.

"Hurrah for me," Paul spouted.

"While I, on the other hand, resemble closely her first love."

"First real love," Judy corrected.

"How long ago?" Paul asked,

"You mean Big Ron?"

"No, the first love."

"Years now."

"How many?"

"Over three."

"And you're still hung up on him," Paul said rather dejectedly.

"I probably will be for the rest of my life, Paul, but that's my problem. I don't love you, but you don't love me. We are good friends and sexual partners. That is enough for me, and I thought it was for you too."

"Oh, it is; I'm not complaining," Paul assured Judy.

PAUL, THE MAGNANIMOUS

Paul had signaled the waiter, who was also the cook and the *taverna*'s owner, to bring more carafes of wine and *tsipouro*; he would put the extras on a separate tab and pay for it himself.

An hour ago, this night had been like many others: the friends had gathered to share a simple feast. But the telegram had arrived, and from its short message, he had felt the beginning of an end. An end of what, he did not yet know, but a pall had fallen over his immediate future. He could afford being generous in the spirit of a condemned man who bequeaths his possessions.

Paul looked around the room and remarked to himself again how cleverly the restaurateur, Phillipos, had cobbled together his place of business. Obviously, he had started with a small *souvlaki* stand that had been expanded by removing the rubble of a collapsing building on one side and, on the other, nicely paving the broken-up sidewalk that the city had no money to repair with grouted slabs of slate, but narrowing it at the same time to give more space for tables and chairs and then roofing over the expropriated space with wooden supporting beams covered by thatched bamboo rods. The previous stand had become his kitchen. and his quaint eatery was known for the low prices of its simple, well-prepared, and tasty dishes.

Phillipos was in sync with the tenor of the times: nothing was wasted; there was nothing to waste, no surplus, and for many, not even necessities. Survivable poverty was the great majority's state.

Used, bent nails were straightened, loose string was wound into balls, perishable food was bought and consumed the same day —who had a refrigerator?—and patched clothing served generations—there was nothing to recycle; there was no waste, because ingenuity abounded.

The *santouri* player, Yeros, the old man, they called him, was over ninety. His instrument was considerably older, yet every evening, he set out to the restaurants around the central square and in the surrounding area to play for his nourishment. Since the foreign Anafiotikans had begun patronizing the *taverna*, he had taken a rest from his peripatetic ways and sat in one corner and played all evening, stopping only to eat and drink his gratuities.

Paul considered himself blessed. Living with Judy was a rush; she was always ahead of him. As she was female and older, of course, his lag showed. He was meeting students at university his own age who had lived through war, occupation, civil war, but still had hope even after losing the academic year, as the government had closed the university in retaliation for student demonstra-

tions and demands. He had a close circle of friends that had just
been enlarged by the arrival of Hakim and Sue, who'd also brought
children for the first time into their midst. Such diverse characters
had been bound into intimate exchange, the one-for-all and the all-
for-one loving family: Jason, who looked like a Naxian marble
bust of Socrates with scars, and Cleopatra, who inflamed the beauty of her namesake, and the flaming redheaded dynamo of Little
Ann, and the tall and ethereal Phyllis, the duchess, who enjoyed
cabbage salad with the peons, and others and more, but it was all
ending; his mother's arrival the next day was, he feared, he knew,
but could not accept, at least not with grace, the first brake on his
roll. Even if his father hadn't short-circuited an extension of his deferment, the closure of the university meant that he had no results
upon which to seek a second, so the army was looming. Which
army was the question. If he chose the Greek army, it would be
like swallowing lit dynamite and being blown out into a different
life. If he chose the American, life as nominally known in the
States would gobble him up; good-bye Bohemian. His third choice
was to take the dive his father's friend had offered: a permanent 4-
F classification that guaranteed the dead would be called to duty
before the 4-Fers were. He wanted to stay in Greece whatever the
consequences. Damn the future; now was the time. He had fought
since he was six to lift the lead cap off his mind, and finally, it was
pressing less, not squeezing his brain as tightly, lifting its weight
from his thought and spine. He had been half alive for so long, but
finally, he could begin to fill himself, and the Greek Way was his
choice cuisine.

And the language! God, how he loved the language even if
it wasn't his. Fate had birthed him into English. English, you could
learn, Greek, you had to live from the womb. It was so large and so
easily made new words—it didn't end—and even its action verbs
conveyed psychological nuance. And the writers and the poets, the
Kazantzakis and the Cavafys and the myriad others who kneaded
language into the living bread.

The wine and *tsipouro* had been served, and Jason called
out from the far end of the table as he raised his filled glass high
and said, "Thank you, Paul, the magnanimous."

"You are very welcome, Jason, but I'm Paul, the curtailed, as of tomorrow."

JOHN P., THE ABSENT

"If you want to curtail something, cut that prick's dick off."

"Whose prick?" Little Ron asked, but he knew whom Big Ron meant and agreed with him entirely, the two homophobes of the group. "Not only do I have to sculpt the bust of his buttfucker, I have to do the boy's penis as well." Making a fist with thumb at right angles, Little Ron indicated Little Ann. "She doesn't have to do the work, but she made the arrangements for me to do it."

"My goodness, aren't the big and little Rons being bitchy," Little Ann observed.

"Bitchy, huh, I'll show you bitchy. I want you there every moment I'm modeling his thing so that queen doesn't get any ideas about me."

"Hey," Big Ron continued, ignoring Little Ann, "I've got an idea for you. Couldn't you fit him a rubber—I mean, he'd put it on himself—and get his groin area suspended between, let's say, two chairs, and then have him lower his tool in a bucket of plaster that you mixed to set up quick, and you could have Little Ann tickling his ass to keep him erect."

Little Ann threw a tomato slice at Big Ron.

"Just a suggestion."

HAKIM, THE RASTAFARIAN

"Ouh, I lovez sug-ges-tions," Hakim tossed out as he and Sue entered the *taverna.*

"Hakim, Sue, come in! Join us! Here, we'll add two chairs," Jason exclaimed. He had befriended the couple warmly within the hour of Hakim's belated arrival in Anafiotika two weeks previously.

When Hakim wanted to be understood, he cobbled key words into his running stream of French and Spanish clips to make sense. No one could imitate his speech patterns, because they changed with the wind, riding a voice of humor.

Jason considered Hakim to be a fellow criminal, not a violent one as he had been, and always funny, but still a lowlife brother.

Hakim loved everybody, smoked dope, and praised life.

SUE, THE JOYFULL

Life was the whole for Sue; she needed nothing else and wanted nothing more. Her son, she had left in the care of *Κυρία Σόφια*, who loved looking after the chocolate fledgling. But her daughter was too young to be far from her mother, and Sue carried her in a breast pouch.

"You look down, Paul," Sue observed.

"Yeah, my mother arrives from the States tomorrow."

"But that should be the cause of great joy."

6: THE TRUCE

Paul was questioning his sanity. He was actually getting along with his mother. He even liked her a little. They didn't argue, and they talked like real people, actually exchanging information. To what else could he ascribe this change—change, nothing—metamorphosis in his mother's behavior except to assigning the hell-on-heels aspect of her character to his father's encouragement, or at least support, but that made no sense, certainly not consciously, for his father was the target of the greater part of her peccadilloes and peculiarities. At times, Paul had been the scorekeeper in his parents' battles. His father was mainly and mostly polite; his mother was not above a kick to the nuts, but out of tenderness for Paul's reduced state, she only boxed her son's ears. When dealing with the "others," Jane was condescending to the world yet responsively aware of its slightest criticism. Notwithstanding, here was Jane, getting along with Judy like friends from the very beginning of time.

The four of them met often—Mary, of course always along —for meals and concerts and museums and, minus Paul, for shopping. Paul had to drink too much *tsipouro* to sober up at all. Mary was no longer advising him. She was in shock. She started making her cross more often and looked up to heaven at each opportunity, certain that an awesome spirit was near—the sun's halo had never faded.

They four went to Mykonos together, and then to Zakynthos to meet Mary's architect and give their views on the house plans. Their pairing in everything was Paul/Mary, Judy/Jane, who walked arm in arm!

Paul was wiped out. A lifetime of opinion—well, most of it —upended like the monster wave that had capsized Jason's trawler. He was praying that his sudden, unexpected moments—no, not of dizziness per se, but of panic—were the result of too much sun and drink and not his brain suffering another concussion from banging against the concrete of his conceits. Probably the simplest explanation was the best: Jane had fallen under the magic of Greece, and her rush to succeed had been replaced by the pleasure of being. And she had begun actually listening to Paul talk of a different way of life with different goals. She genuinely admired Paul's desire to take up a way of living that aspired to fill the inner person with the possessions that belonged to all, like love and beauty, rather than crowd the outer person with things and stuff that obscured the view lying beyond them. She dared to harbor an exceedingly small hope that Paul might join the church, marry before ordination, and father many grandchildren through his naturally Greek wife for the joy of her and John's later years. The problem with that wish, however, was that as a priest, he could not also be a businessman, a hotelier. Returning quickly, however, to the present, she was captivated by Judy's English, how rich and melodic her conversation was, and she was delighted by Judy's command and love of Greek, and she was impressed by Judy's objectivity and knowledge of the world and its mores. The chaff didn't have a place in her thoughts: Judy was now a captivating *femme totale*, not *fatale*; she was no longer —and, upon reflection, had never been—a gold-digging foreign slut.

Paul was spooked. One brace in the logical structure of his constructed world evaporated, and the entire edifice of his thought collapsed. He suddenly became the loneliest man on the planet; no one else had ever been so wrong. He was in danger. All of the work he had done on his botched brain to regain at least nominal use seemed like a comic book now, and just as real.

He had to get away. Hakim was his savior; every time Paul returned to Anafiotika, the non-stop jive man calmed him down. But the cure for Paul's confusion, not just its symptoms, was beyond even Hakim.

* * *

"You know, Dad is very tired," Jane said.

Paul saw his fate click in line like a self-assembling erector set.

"Why more now?" Paul asked. "He could retire if he wanted, but he doesn't. I know that. He's told me that he plans to go out in his boots, so to speak, working."

"Yes, he loves work," Jane agreed, "but he also needs periods for rest; he's only human. He hasn't taken a real vacation since we got back from Greece in '56."

For anyone who could not subtract, "That's six years," she added.

Paul's next lurch would be a déjà vu—no, not the repeat of something that had happened before, but rather a reaction that had been pre-programmed from the beginning. Was there no way out? Had Anafiotika and other friends simply been the illusions of an extended dream? Was his resolution to stay in Greece and change his fate like a New Year's flake? He knew he would say what he didn't want to say for a reason that appeared to be primordial.

"What if I went back and relieved him?" Paul asked, the dutiful son who was not yet an independent man.

"Oh, would you, Paul! That would be lovely. And it would give Dad a chance to meet Judy. Oh, it's such a perfect plan, Paul. Thank you so much."

Concussion upon concussion; beyond having become sociable and agreeable, Jane had said, "Thank you!" To him! To her son! To Paul, the dumb bunny!

But wait! Had he actually volunteered or only mused?

But wait! Did any decision he might take make a damned bit of difference? The tension in the world had been at a crisis level since the failed Bay of Pigs invasion the preceding year. Serious trouble was brewing between the Cold War adversaries, and it pivoted around Cuba. No side wanted to back down, and the choice was to raise the stakes as high as possible before calling the hand. Paul was aware of current events; in Greece, he was exposed to the many points of view diverse people held.

And yet, even further behind his filial loyalty, one source of Paul's essence germinated: "Get it before it gets you."

War seemed inevitable. He, Paul, could change nothing, en-
lighten no one, nor retard a single little finger on the proverbial
buttons. Ergo, join the fray! Heil testosterone; it made him seek
pussy and give danger the finger.

But wait! The equation had even more elements. There was
also the nurture. How often he had tried shirking responsibility for
himself by claiming never to have been asked or to have never
wanted to be born in the first place. (His father's reaction, "What
means that?" always irked him.) The fact was that he had been
born and therefore wasn't prepared to not have been born except as
an excuse. So, yes, John and Jane, mother and father, had taken ex-
ceptionally good care of him, providing everything he might need
and more, and neither of them were responsible for his nasty knock
on the head. Not John, who'd ordered a family car based on business considerations, nor Jane, who could not have caught him as he
was being flung from the car even if she had been paying attention.
No, he'd done it to himself by showing off to Susie.

But in summation, for all that good fortune of his youth he
had enjoyed, he owed something back; Socrates had drunk the
hemlock, so surely, he could stomach the U.S., Arkansas, Hot
Springs, the DeSoto Hotel?

But wait! Going back was an adventure; if the current
knockabout was ending, a new one was beginning, and to see that,
he only had to look in different directions.

But wait! The whole thing went back much further than any
individual. There was the ancient tradition of family unity and the
succession of power from parent to child, as he would have complete control over the business for three months. In the past, they
had entrusted their enterprise to him for days at a time, even ten,
but never for months. And then there was the coming war. Sure,
there was always a lot of tension in the world. No one seemed con-
tent that seventy million people of all ages had been slaughtered in
the last war, and they courted even more death and destruction.
Which side was right, which wrong, or could the future of humanity lie only in the temporary point of view of this little side and man
or that?

And there was also the morbid fascination he felt to experience the legal savagery of being bound to one woman, a trait that might have been older even than the human species. Another ancient imperative was duty to the tribe or nation. But if he went back, he was also deciding on joining the American army, as he would be unable to return to Greece without a deferment to validate his passport.

But wait! These thoughts were a bag of balls. There were only two ways that a person could live, either in the fold or out of it. Paul had wanted out, but he had just volunteered to re-immerse himself in his nemesis—or mused on doing so.

He couldn't even beat himself over his internal schisms with Judy to arbitrate. Without warning, she suddenly began expecting him to be a man, in command, sure of himself, making logical, step-by-step decisions, and she would not allow him to wobble, especially if he were thinking of marriage. She had lost faith in Paul's judgment when she'd found Jane so very different from his description.

In all the banter and comradery between Jane and Judy, anything relating to matrimony remained undiscussed by silent mutual consent. That omission emptied Paul's space enough for him to breath.

Jane offered to supplement his cash to upgrade to a first-class ticket, but Paul refused, rightly believing that going to hell in style cursed him to stay there forever.

Judy summed up the situation: "Go back and let your father come over. He sounds like a wonderful man. I'll keep them entertained so they will have less time to worry about you, or what we intend, or don't intend, to do. I am not in a hurry to marry you and, certainly even less, anyone else."

"Except the first-love guy," Paul could not resist a jab.

"Leave that," Judy replied defensively. "I was saying, and it makes sense, to do your national service over there. Our friends here have described how rough the Greek army is, how easy it is to land in jail for a week, or a month, for minor transgressions—minor, at least, to us. Plus, the pay is a hundred drachmas a month, only five times what you make for an hour lesson. Maybe the

American army will station you in Europe. Since you speak the language, you could even be sent right back here."

Judy's probably right, Paul mused as he was walking through the Plaka back to Anafiotika from Monastiraki, but he sensed that she also may have been expressing the desire to have a mate, in whatever arrangement, who had enough money to make her—their—life more carefree. As a soldier in the Greek army, he might look to her for support rather than enlarge their resources; two together got along better on a double income than one alone on a single, but a hundred drachmas per month wouldn't even buy his cigarettes if he smoked commercial brands rather than the army's handouts.

* * *

At the next corner, commotion was in progress. Paul was ascending the wide stairway that intersected a pedestrian walk twenty meters ahead. There were *tavernas* on all four corners, which was an unusual concentration even in the Plaka, which was known for its many eateries and bars. There were lengths of "Do Not Cross This Line" tape fluttering here and there; no Greek would be stopped by such a flimsy barricade, and a number had torn through the taped-off area even before it was finished. A few police officers were trying to clear the intersection of interested parties who wanted to get closer to see what was occurring. Fire department men were wrestling with a large hose they were connecting to a fire hydrant. A large black camera was supported by a complex tripod-dolly mechanism. Paul read the action board: "IN THE COOL OF THE NIGHT TAVERN SCENE TAKE FIVE." The scene coordinator was shouting through a megaphone, ordering the frame area cleared and the water hose opened. A huge tarp had been spread out high above the action area, and the stream of water was aimed to fall on it and, through many tiny holes, drip like drizzle. A cab entered on the pedestrian walk from the left. A doorman darted out of the entrance to the *taverna* on the back-right side. The door of the cab opened, and out stepped Jane Fonda wearing an English Fog-style dark--beige trench coat, her hair wrapped in a head scarf. She was immediately shielded by the doorman's monstrous umbrella, which was held high, and she dashed within the *taverna*. "Cut and wrap," the director announced, also on a bullhorn.

Paul was stunned. It was all so fake! First, who in their right mind would believe a drizzling rain in Athens in the summer —maybe once in a decade, but surely unrelated to the story unless it was meant to set a dreary mood; a hyped symbol for tears, perhaps? Then the taxi on the pedestrian walk, how did it get there? No roads, only walkways led to it. But if a taxi was so necessary, this meant that the particular *taverna* was irreplaceable, but it wasn't; Paul had taken his females there for dinner, and Judy had remarked that it might be too rustic to suit Jane and Mary. That was it, he decided, its rusticness, but they hadn't shot a scene from inside, or was there another camera crew doing the interior? No one was coming out of the *taverna*, probably indicating in fact that shooting was occurring.

Paul walked on up the pedestrian stairway toward Anafiotika. Six months previously, in the fall, he had answered a casting call. The notice had appeared in the *Athens News*, a daily rag in English with lots of notices and classified ads, especially those of the American military contingent who were rotating stateside or on to another foreign assignment and wanted to sell their belongings; unfortunately, the appliances were all 110-volt.

John P. read the notice and told them about it. "I'm going, of course; they'll need me. After all, I am an actor by profession, and I have an ample and beautifully done dossier of my work.

"I hope it is an American and not a British film company; the Yanks pay better, and I don't have to put up with the silliness of English snobbery," he continued.

"Wait, John," interjected Nick, who rarely spoke. "The small print states that all cast members must speak two of three languages, English plus Greek or Turkish, Levantine appearance preferred. You don't fit."

"Oh, silly boy, I'll make myself up to look like the queer Sultan himself."

"But John, were there any homosexual sultans, what with all the harems and such?" Judy asked dryly.

"And John, you don't speak much Greek," Paul observed.

"Only gutter talk," Little Ron added.

"Oh dears, dears," John P. began as he stretched out his chin and sucked in his stomach, "you are all being daft. Talent is what they want, and that I have talent in surplus is obvious. I was much sought after by the best directors for leading rolls in England.

"In any case, I'm answering the call, and I am confident that I shall have more than a walk-on presence. That's what they are asking for, isn't it, Nick? I mean, it does say walk-ons and extras. But when they see my screen test, they will replace one of the leads with me."

"Male or female," Little Ron twittered.

"But they rest of you should go. No, not you, Little Ron, unless they're looking for ape-like midgets."

"A queer calls me a midget and an ape? That's the day. Screw off!"

"Not you either, Big Ron; no amount of makeup could wash the Irish out of you.

"You, Nick, would be the one most sought after me, if they want a pretty boy. I certainly do.

"Jason, you are too old; their insurance won't cover you.

"And you, Paul, granted, you don't have any charisma, but you speak two of their three languages, and you look the swarthy part, so maybe they would use you in backgrounds, for local color.

"And as for you, ladies, I need say nothing," John P. concluded.

"That we should be so lucky," Little Ann piped.

* * *

The three of them had answered the call. The setting was the Rex Theater, the beautiful art deco mini-skyscraper of Athens located between Omonia and Syntagma Squares on University Avenue.

"The two of you boys just follow my lead," John P. said to Nick and Paul as he motioned them to be seated in an anteroom and then began righting himself. First, he checked that his hair was neat. Then he sent a small tremor through his body and straightened himself from his usual lascivious slouch to a John Wayne ramrod, and then he began rearranging his facial features to appear an older but distinguished man, and finally, he disappeared through one of the back doors.

"What do you think he's up to?" Paul asked. "They told all of us to take numbers and wait in here, and we are many."

Nick had nothing to add and said nothing.

About every ten minutes, a number was called, and the designee exited the anteroom for the stage through a side door. John P. returned just as the fourth hopeful was presenting himself.

"We will wait to the end," John P. announced.

"Why, we have numbers?" Paul protested. "Three or four guys came in after us, and there could still be many more."

"Nevertheless, we will wait to go in last; first, I will go. Then Nick and then you, Paul."

"Why?" Paul insisted again.

"Because I have arranged that we three be interviewed by the man himself."

"And who's that?"

"None other than Elia Kazan," John P. reported with great, solemn fanfare.

"He is a fine director," Nick affirmed.

"So, did you also learn what the film's going to be called?"

"Yes, I have, but this is between us only," John P. said conspiratorially, in the same low tone of voice he had used in speaking the director's name. "It is titled *America, America*."

"Oh, shit!" Escaped Paul

"Why should you object to your history?" Nick asked.

"It's not that I object, but it's probably another immigrant story, and I've heard hundreds, well, tens anyway, no, hundreds," Paul explained.

"Oh, you immigrants are everywhere."

"But John, you've been living in Greece for years. What do you call yourself?"

"Silly boy, Paul, but then how would you know? An Englishman is always an honored guest, never an immigrant."

111

"I'm sure Little Ron would be happy to hear you say that after you implied that his forebears were a good deal less than Englishmen."

"We are not talking about exceptions to the rule here," John P. replied, and then he ended the conversation by arising and walking around the room as if he were a younger Churchill.

When they were the last three in the anteroom and John P. was next in line to be interviewed, he said, "Dears, you know I really need to do this. It would be a boost to my flagging spirit." But as time counted down to his turn, John P. seemed to grow nervous, and for moments, he reverted to his languid postures. The door opened, and he pulled himself together and marched through to his certain and glorious fate.

"Signs of being a real person show through him at times," Nick observed.

"Yeah," Paul agreed, "when he stops acting, he's okay. I wonder what he'll be like in there, the person or the actor?"

"If he is a person, he might well get a part, but if he's the actor, stage door exit," Nick concluded.

Thereafter, they were silent until the door opened again. Paul wished Nick well and settled back to await his turn.

When it came, Paul walked through the door onto the wings of the great stage. At the far end, he saw a person sitting in shadow several meters away from a folding-type metal chair that was positioned under a strong and restricted shaft of light. He did the obvious, walking to the chair and sitting down. Immediately, his vision was constricted within the cone of light; he could see nothing on the dark stage or in the theater beyond.

"You are number forty-three," a male voice said from beyond Paul's vision but easily within his hearing.

"Well." Paul answered, "I'm not number forty-three; it was given to me as the number of my turn for an interview." Then it occurred to Paul that his answer might have sounded foppish, but he didn't take it back or amend it in the next moments of silence.

"In either case," the voice continued, "the personal information you gave upon application for an interview will be found in a file labeled 'Forty-three.'"

"Fair enough," Paul replied, but what else could he say.

"You look Greek. Are you?"

"Yes, father and mother."

"But your accent is decidedly American, midwestern."

"I was born in the States, both of them here."

"And how well do you speak Greek?"

"Tolerably to good, but by no means perfect. I've also studied Ancient Greek, and I'm now enrolled in philology studies at the University of Athens."

"So, you are fond of Greece?"

"Passionately!"

"Why?"

"Because it is so real. Life is hard, but no one makes excuses, and everyone is responsible for themselves. And then, of course, there's the extended family that is much larger here than there, and wiser and stronger as people than I am, and yet I'm the one who had all the opportunities—that may not make a lot of sense, but I feel the disparity between the haves and the have nots, and the have nots win. And then the sea and sun and food and joy and pain and, and everything. Plus, I've been to places, both on islands and the mainland, where I swear I can feel the life of the planet reaching, spreading, flowing out from the ground. And the ruins make you realize that if such an advanced society as Periclean Athens could be destroyed in its time, isn't it possible that the same could happen to us in ours."

"Of course it is. I think the foundational principle of fine art is to awaken the consciousness of all to the recognition of others."

Paul couldn't meld what he had said to the director's observation, but it was a worthy statement itself. "You mean to say to see the other in the same scale, not always 'me first!'"

"The constant appreciation of who and what and why and where and how...

"Enough of that. Do you have any acting experience?"

"Very little, just three plays in college and a leading role in only one."

"Which play?"

"*Christ in Concrete City.*"

"Yes, Turner's work."

"We modified it slightly."

"How?"

"It's written for four males and two females, but we made it two and two."

"Did you have props?"

"None. In fact, we only used the stage in front of the main curtain."

"And costumes?"

"None. Our street clothes. Well, the women wore long skirts, but the other guy and I wore our jeans."

"How was the play received?"

"We got good reviews in the college media, and the second night, we got a standing ovation. But that was it, two nights, Friday and Saturday."

"Did you have a director?"

"No, we directed ourselves. The other three were drama students. I was the only outsider."

"What was your major?"

"Ancient Greek in the beginning, but then I switched to English literature and composition."

"Why?"

"The professor had been using the same textbooks for forty-three years—strange, there's that number again—and he was so bored we sometimes had to wake him. There was no other choice; he was the only Greek professor there. There were two other old guys in the classical language department, but they were both Latinists. And then the Erasmian pronunciation they used was dreadful and, in the end, unendurable. Later, I learned that rough breathing was no longer—but I'm wandering off subject," Paul admitted.

"Yes, I see. Well, let's sum up: you look the part because you are. You have limited acting experience but possibly of high quality. You speak two languages, but it's unlikely that you would have a speaking role, as those are mostly filled, but it helps in understanding stage directions that will be in Greek and English. I'm only saying that you have passed the first cut, but there will be others.

"One other thing. would you shave off your mustache?"

Paul was nonplussed. He'd guessed that most of the males in the film would reflect an Eastern Mediterranean background, and that was heavily peppered with mustaches. He hesitated in answering, remembering instead the first time he had been obliged to shave his mustache and beard.

He had returned to Arkansas in September from his second, but first solo, trip to Greece during the summer of 1959. At nineteen and two months, his beard was a scraggly mess, but it was a first step toward the look he wanted for himself. James Dean had died four years previously, but in his short acting career, he had made the outsider the man to be. Still, at the time, facial hair was reserved for the outcasts.

Paul had been without money since Madrid, where he had arrived eight days before with twenty-five dollars, which, after the fourth day, had been spent to the last peseta, but he had a ticket to Hot Springs, standby from Madrid to New York to Memphis and, finally, to ground zero. He had lived off the sympathy of the TWA stewardesses at the airport, who had given him meal vouchers for breakfast and dinner when the day passed with no cancellations. During the hours after the last possible flight for the day, he'd wandered around parts of the city using the airline's free bus transportation to come and go. He'd taken the last bus back to the airport, where the stewardesses had also supplied him with blankets and pillows and arranged with the cleanup staff to allow him to sleep on a couch in the waiting room. Everything he'd eaten for four days had been free airline fare. On the fourth day, there'd been a cancellation, and Paul had boarded the TWA Constellation for seventeen hours of flight. Finally arriving in Hot Springs, he could have pleaded the use of a phone at the local airport and called his parents to come and pick him up, or he could have taken a cab and had the driver wait until he went into the hotel and got money to pay the fair. He had decided on the latter course, as he was certain his parents would rather pay the taxi than take time away from business. If they had known when he would arrive, they would have met him at the airport, but as he was flying standby, arrival time was not possible to predict.

Even as the cab was pulling into the diagonal parking unloading space in front of the DeSoto, Paul saw his father within, and he knew that his dad had seen him, changed directions, and was coming out to greet him. But he was mistaken; his father went around to the driver's side and said, "I don't know where you pick up that bum, but take him from here."

"Hey, Dad, it's me, Paul."

"What?" his father barked back. "You no Paul."

"Mister, whoever he is, he owes three dollars and forty-three cents cab fare, and I only brought him because he promised you'd pay it."

"Yes, yes, here," John said and handed the cabbie a five. "Keep change," he said totally chagrined. Then, turning to his son, he continued, "Paul, is that you? What have you done to you? I thought you are bum, and I come out to send you away. Quick, go upstairs. Shave before Mother see you."

For the first and only time during a reunion, John did not embrace Paul and kiss his checks.

"I'm not going to shave, Dad. I'm growing a beard."

"Oh, yes you ares" and "Oh, no I'm nots" followed in rapid succession until Jane joined the fray, and the battle lasted a week. They had insisted that he enter the hotel from the back and not come down from their in-hotel apartment that, fortunately, had a direct outside door—under no circumstances was he to appear in the public spaces of the hotel. And as his father's health deteriorated by the day with powerful health bulletins announced frequently by his mother, Paul decided at the end of the week to shave.

His image would have to wait until he was twenty-one.

Thus, Paul was not in sync with anyone asking him to shave his now bushy stash for any reason.

"No," he answered.

"Thank you for your honesty, but your refusal means you don't make the first cut after all," the great director said.

"Why?" Paul asked, but he was not surprised. He also felt that Nick and John P. would be cut for different reasons in a future culling, and they were.

"Making a movie is a collaborative undertaking, and direction given must be executed—obviously, in a safe manner regardless the demand. I'm—no director would—not going to say cut off your nose for the part, but if I say, 'beard,' you shouldn't wait for the barber, understand."

* * *

Yes, Paul did, and no, he didn't understand both then and epecially now. Where was Mary Pappas when he needed her?

She had suggested Jane use reverse psychology on him, and therefore, she should give him a clue as to how he should really nail his mother for her infernal and eternal interference in his affairs. He knew Mary was on Zakynthos, building her home. Paul would have to travel by boat, land, and boat again, two days at least, probably three, to get Mary's advice, even if the last time they had confided, she had admitted to astonishment and had failed to give any guidance.

He needed advice, someone's advice; he would write to Emerald and Jimmy. Maybe they could see things more clearly than he.

He searched his memory for his exact words when he'd offered to relieve his father. He had only said, "What if . . .?"

But wait! When did answers turn irrelevant and questions become rhetorical?

7: HURRIED LETTERS

"Dear Emerald and Jimmy," Paul began. Judy, Jane and Mary were shopping and bonding, thus giving him a few hours to reconstruct his mind.

I'm writing the same letter to both of you because the question I need immediate help in answering is the same.

I am undone. How's that for being Shakespearian, or anti-Shakespearian? But seriously, of everything I know, or knew, the bottom has dropped away, the top has flown to the moon, and the sides have been blown to bits. I can't believe this change of personality that my mother evinces. She has even stopped wiping all the silverware and glassware at the common restaurants we frequent. She talks to me as a human being rather than from somewhere between a slave and its master. She likes Judy! They can't get enough of each other's company. She laughs, she drinks enough wine to get silly, and everything pleases her. From the fourth day after her arrival, she has criticized nothing. What's happened? Am I the sow's ear become a silk purse? Or has a new reality slipped into the universe? What's going on? What's Dad say? Jimmy, you would know that better than Emerald. I know they talk by phone; has he said anything about a change in what she says?

Not only undone, but nailed as well. I posed a hypothetical question about coming back to relive Dad, and she gloomed onto it as if my tentative offer was a postscript of the Ten Commandments.

Help!

I don't understand.

Am I wandering in the wilderness?

But I can't ask you to be my spies and informers without an Anafiotika installment.

This one begins with my friend, Jason, and ends with my buddy, Hakim.

Since Jason and Phyllis began living together, they also started a collaboration to write Jason's soldier of fortune experiences as a series for television. Jason related, and Phyllis recorded. Nothing remarkable until you consider that she wrote in shorthand. How does a duchess of the Crown know shorthand? Unbelievable, but true. Anyway, as soon as they had finished three episodes, Jason sent them off to an acquaintance at the BBC. The channel accepted the three pilot episodes and commissioned twelve more for a total of fifteen and hinted that more might be wanted. Jason was ecstatic; after a long life of making dirty money, he was about to become an honest man. Phyllis was thrilled; not only would she be able to put off returning to England, she also truly loves Jason—who is old enough to be her grandfather, but in no other way—and they have a feisty sex life if their sounds and noises mean anything, with Phyllis obviously doing most of the work.

They planned a party to celebrate their good fortune, scheduled weeks hence so that Jason's old underworld cronies could travel to Athens from various parts of the planet, mainly the Middle East, North Africa, and Latin American. In the time between the acceptance of their work and the party to celebrate it, Hakim and Sue arrived in our midst. I think I've told you about them already, so I won't repeat myself. Hakim and Jason became immediate fast friends, and Jason shaved his beard, cut his hair short, lost weight, and is now filled with energy. I mean, he was taking us all on field trips from close by on the other side of the Acropolis, on Mars Hill, where Paul spoke to the Areopagus—he is particularly interested in the Disciple Paul and intends to use part of his earnings from the series to retrace the paths that Paul followed during his four journeys from the Holy Land, culminating in Rome. We've gone out of Athens to Epidavros and Olympia and Delphi. The man is indefatigable, and he knows a great deal about many things, and he's especially a history buff. But Jason and Phyllis didn't stop working; they were finishing new episodes. Of course, there was a common theme in all the stories. That was our payment for Jason's cultural guidance: we listened to the scripts and made comments. The hero—but since he was a knave, the dark hero—always started the adventure in a blaze of action, not so much death and destruction as clever plans and shady dealings. About two-thirds through, the momentum began turning against the protagonist, but the resistance only caused him to delve deeper into the human dilemma the story portrayed. And the end was always an escape that barely succeeded on one end, but that opened the other for the next story. I'm really impressed with their work.

By the day of the party, only two of Jason's friends had come. Apparently, the others had either died of old age, been killed in various schemes, or were languishing in prisons. But no matter, there were plenty of local friends.

Jason had asked me to be the barman and bought the 90-proof alcohol and fruit juices that he would mix up into his favorite rowdy-making punch. He and I had just begun our punch brewing when Judy arrive and told Jason that Phyllis needed to see him immediately. All the women had collected at Nick and Cleopatra's to assemble and don the customs that female characters in Jason's adventures had worn. Cleo was the belly dancer, Little Ann, the underage daughter of a friend, etc., but Judy, the whore in Marseilles, was dressed in street clothes, so Phyllis dispatched her to bring Jason back in response to a telegram that had just arrived.

Jason went off grumbling, leaving me in charge of finishing the punch. True, I taste-tested as I went, but I swear it was from the fumes, but whatever, I got so drunk I literally fell under the table. That's where Judy found me when she came back to tell me the news and that the party had not been called off due to the cancellation of all the episodes, including the first three, but would instead go on as a wake for integrity, since the food and drink had been paid for and the *taverna* rented. I understood very little. She had not seen how wasted I was because her attention was elsewhere. Finally, she realized that I was not goofing off but totally drunk, and she consented to take me back home because I was useless for anything other than lying in bed and trying to puke in the pail.

Judy left. I was lying in bed except that it had a large number of rapidly shifting axes. But was I lying or flying or spinning or all? Time passed, I guess, and I was getting drunker and drunker but not sick, since most of my inebriation had come from fumes and I had eaten bread and cheese—you know, to clear the palate between sips.

Hakim entered, sat on the side of the bed, and shifted me to sit up against the headboard. Then he told me to toke on the joint he had placed between my lips, and he said, "Had boss-man hep afur you. U'just drunk. He be down," or something to that effect. Anyway, we went back to the party. The dope had sobered me—or knocked me beyond the pale of drunkenness. We all, including Jason, had a good time for a sad cause.

So, you see, life's not all fun and games, even here, and I'm depending on you two to fill me in.

Am I suffering a "Jason and the BBC?"

* * *

Within ten days of sending his letter Paul received a reply, remarkably fast mail service for the times.

"Dear Paul," it began. That was good; at least they had not addressed him as fallen comrade.

> We are joining in a single reply and will mail it express, with each of us giving his and her report on your situation.
>
> I, Emerald, go first.
>
> My friend, I fear you are being set up, but at the same time, you should know that my knowledge is limited to Mom's reports and out of date by two months and more. Mary suggested that your mother use reverse psychology on you; her intent was not to injure you but to shock Jane, who had been obsessing with anyone who would listen about the grave mistakes you were contemplating. The pivot was that you really only wanted to play around with sex and cohabitation but had no intention of getting serious with Judy, and thus, the suggestion to marry her would bring you to your senses.
>
> I am also surprised by your mother's change of character, but I can offer no insight except to say that Jane was beginning to consider Mary's suggestion as being plausible by the time they left Hot Springs.
>
> I've decided on the University of Chicago and will be leaving soon. Stavros is already there and has found an apartment for us close to campus.

Jimmy is next.

Emerald.

Paul, nothing has changed from what I can gather. Both of your parents, regardless how one or the other may be acting now, are still totally committed to assist you in returning to the U.S., marrying a Greek-American girl, making many grandchildren, and running the business for them. No, one thing has changed, and I believe it is what you are seeing in your mother's behavior: they have decided to deal with you in a more adult manner and less as a pliable child.

Now that you know, will we be seeing you soon?

Look at it this way: you are still young, but you have had a good time for almost a year. That's more than most people get in a lifetime.

On the subject of burning your bridges by joining the Greek army, I vote no.

Jimmy.

* * *

Armed with this new information, Paul was no better off than he had been before. But why? It should have steeled his resolve to follow his own mind, but it didn't; in fact, it had the opposite effect. His newfound self-confidence eroded, not completely, but too much for bold action. But why? *But why?* Were his plans so extreme that his parents thought subterfuge was necessary for dealing with him? He wasn't bright, he knew that, but he was managing in the world, and he had finished a bachelor's degree at a good university, if more by assiduous labor and a few good ideas rather than by mental alacrity. Sure, his brain had been knocked about, but the accident had happened so many years ago, and he could no longer use it—to himself, or to others—as his excuse for his failings. He feared a personal deficiency that was more obvious to others than to himself. If he could see where he went wrong . . . but that too was stupid. Everyone wanted to understand their mistakes so that they would not repeat the same errors. All of his Anafiotika friends were cleverer than him, the women obviously, even Little Ann. Maybe not Nick; no one know what he thought, Rather, Nick had attained the wisdom of silence, but it could also be a dodge. And Paul's parents obviously considered him to be but slightly above a fruit basket nut case. How could he ignore their assessments? They held their version of his good as the beacon of their efforts, past—how many times had both of them said, "We are doing this all for you"?—and presently via the rarefied mechanism of reverse psychology, and into the future if there was no compelling reason for it to differ from the foregoing. Through him, they would arise from peasant/artisan backgrounds to aggrandizing citizens of the greatest country on earth. (As if everyone didn't believe their home nation was wonderful in its way.) But for all their grandstanding, they were good people, his father especially. Even his mother; although he detested her, he admired her. She had energy. She overflowed with ideas, some of which were good, if usually impractical. She was generous in personal time and material support to all those she felt were deserving, even to a few questionable cases. Her politics were liberal, her cultural sophistication high. She inspired loyalty—maybe fear, maybe the two together—in all who were her equals and under. She had allowed him to do surprising things, like being completely free in the company of his dogs and armed with his rifle to roam their extensive land and the forests beyond for hours, a whole day at a time. And she had agreed to him taking flying lessons at fourteen and getting a pilot's license and flying all over the south-central states before he was old enough to get a driver's license. And she'd recognized that after grade school, while he was mending, he'd needed a better education than he could get in Hot Springs and thus had sent him, mercifully—probably for both—off to out-of-state boarding schools. And she loved animals. Toward his father, he was in constant competition that he always lost. His father was like a flesh-and-blood man of steel. John had worked from early childhood at physically demanding labor-intensive jobs, and his muscles were like stretching bands of steel. He had overcome an episode of rickets disease as a young teenager and now stood as straight and majestic as the

Statue of Liberty. People were naturally drawn to him, women especially for his gentlemanly consideration. (How often Paul had been dragged off by his father to help select a present for Jane because it was their anniversary, her birthday, Valentine's Day, Mother's Day, and every other commemorative event, and John had just remembered, and it was equally in Paul's interest that his mother was happy at not being forgotten.) But men also were attracted to John for his wisdom and shrewdness and diplomacy and steadiness. And Paul admired his father for warding off and slowly dissolving the prejudice against Yankees, immigrants in general, and independent thinkers who were not fond of rabid causes. There was so much weight on their side, the mass of history and experience. Could they be totally wrong? No, that was obvious. But where was he wrong? He wanted a simple life filled with learning and discovery and adventure. He wasn't bright, but he was smart enough to live on little, and he enjoyed taxing himself. No one had ever given him a cogent argument for not reversing the standard theme of the golden years retirement by playing while you were young and working, and hard, if you got old. It made perfect sense to him, but no one else agreed, least of all his parents, and he couldn't understand why they did not. But his thoughts weren't helping, only adding more confusion, and he already had enough of that. But maybe he was looking at the situation wrongly. Maybe there were no decisions to make, just steps to take. The progression had been there from the beginning, the whole growing-up rigmarole, the fascination with sex and the sexy female, and the education challenge, and the constant battle to sustain himself however little he needed, and, lastly but not least, to figure out who he was.

Maybe, Paul decided, *that's a function of time.*

8: OPEN THE DOOR AND THE FLIES SWARM IN

When Paul learned of the setup in progress to continue steering and stirring his ship of person, he mounted a Möbius strip of negative emotion. He went through them all: rage, shame, pity, self-depreciation, self-appreciation, and, of course, the usual batch of love/hate—round and round and round. He couldn't even talk to Judy; she had joined the other camp. Jason was devastated by the cancellation of his soldier of fortune series on BBC, and Phyllis was distracted looking after him, so their consultations were no longer given. Hakim had the solution to everything, and he spoke for Sue: smoke more dope, good, but the problem remained. Nick and Cleopatra were off to Crete for the summer. John P. was John P. and, now without his Teddy, lost in self-loathing and self-pity. The Little's, Ron and Ann, had decamped for Germany, Big Ron for Ireland. Efrat had gone home to Tel Aviv. Even Leslie Jr. had escaped back to the U.S., not that his presence would have made any difference.

Paul was on his own.

But that was his next problem, as he often made stupid mistakes, especially when he was hot and shot with testosterone, as he was now. He needed time to douse his emotional infernos and concentrate with every bit of the mind he still had on what he was about to do; it would have lasting effect.

Everything would. Even doing nothing. But then, that was doing something. The question was one of prescience, but he couldn't see clearly to the end of the day let alone through the fullness of life.

One change was clear: the gloves were off! He had never played tricks on his parents while growing up, having been almost so truthful with them that he was factual. Often, where a little feint or whitish fib would have saved him from punishment, he'd taken the whacks.

No more. Rules changed. Reverse psychology could be reversed, and it could capsize his mother's schemes, and if the sad tale were ever to be referred to in the future, it would be known as Jane's folly.

He likened himself to the defenders of Stalingrad, surrounded by Fascists, but winter was coming. The first freeze would commence the next time he and Jane were alone.

* * *

"We haven't talked about this since you first arrived," Paul began, "but I'll be leaving soon, and we should sort things out now.

"You see how well Judy and I get along, and you said that the hardest part of a relationship was the day by day, everything shared. How would say we stack up?"

"Ah," Jane replied, stalling. She had been hoping that nothing more would be said concerning her suggestion that Paul and Judy marry if they got along living together, but since he was forcing her hand, she had to stay on track. "Yes, I think you get on nicely. But of course, this is an ideal situation. You're both young and aren't burdened down by responsibilities, so it's easy to be together. But in a real relationship, there's no getting around responsibility, especially when the children start arriving."

"That won't be a problem for us for a long time. Judy isn't anxious to become a mother, and I could skip the father bit forever."

Jane was feeling threatened, but she strove not to show her discomfort. Mary's advice to use reverse psychology had been working, Paul had volunteered to relieve John at the DeSoto, and that meant that he was falling in line. She and John would return to Arkansas at the end of November, and Paul would be drafted shortly after the new year—John had seen to that. During his service, he would meet nice Greek girls aplenty; she would see to that. Judy would recede in importance to the role of his playmate in a youthful episode and be effectively forgotten. Granted, she was a nice young woman, and very smart, if not stunningly good looking. But she wasn't Greek. And this was not to single Judy out; Jane applied that discrimination to all of his potential mates.

"Yes, Paul, but remember, accidents happen."

Paul was tempted to answer, "Yeah, but there's always abortion." But if he did, he would be reverting to honesty, and that was *verboten!* "Well, sure, but we're talking about planned events, not accidents."

"Still—"

"I think I can ease your concern; Judy is a sensible woman, and I'm not a dope, so we will act appropriately in any contingency."

"Yes, it does," Jane assured him, and she either believed or had convinced herself that she had not seen a crack in the new Paul toward the old. "I've said this a thousand times, so I'll say it a thousand and one, thank you, Paul, for going back to relieve Dad. You can't imagine how much this means to both of us. Be assured that it means a great deal. When you too are a parent, you will understand more fully what I feel."

"Gotcha," Paul tossed out

"Now you look," Paul said as he passed the binoculars to his mother. "I track them over days." His sunset passion was to look at the sun through binoculars when it was low in the sky and its brightness would not damage the eyes and follow the movement of sunspots in a year of maximal activity.

"There seem to be four of them."

"Count again."

"No, right, five, but are you sure this isn't bad for the eyes."

"When the sun is this low, there's no danger; in fact, it's good for your eyes to bathe them in soft light."

Whoa! He had spoken without thinking, but it was hard getting used to expressing only those thoughts that were held by the majority, and the common belief was that looking at the sun at any angle was bad.

"Have you collected all your things?"

"Well, the books, I'm leaving with Judy, and a few other things, like the binoculars. Most of my clothes, I'm giving to Hakim; I'll get new stuff in the States. I'm going down to Piraeus tomorrow to give Aliki two hundred bucks that I'll say came from Jimmy and then warn him of what I've done so she doesn't thank him before he learns of his generosity."

"That's thoughtful, Paul."

"Well, really, I owe it to her. The agreement was to pay her twenty dollars a month for my keep, but that train trip back and forth ate up three hours a day. Of course, I read on the train, but you know what that's like when you don't have a seat, and if I was lucky enough to get one, within a stop or two, an old person would get on, and if there were no other seats available, I always gave mine."

"That's wonderful, Paul."

For a thought's length, the idea crossed Paul's mind to magnify all his accomplishments to sufficiently inflame his mother's complimenting spirit until the pitch of her approbations caused her to suffer a stroke, but he decided against his conviction—there were no rules in the game, but there were things to be avoided, like parody.

* * *

He boarded the ferry from Mykonos. Judy and Jane were galvanizing each other, and they quickly, if warmly, wished him a good journey. He stayed overnight at Aliki's in Piraeus, rode public transportation to the airport, and ascended the steps to the plane, but before boarding, he paused, turned, inched to the side, and looked over the seacoast and knew that years would pass before he would swim from these beaches again. Then he looked down at the foot of the movable stairwell and remembered kneeling beside the old man at arrival and kissing the ground. He couldn't suck up a kiss in leaving, but he had packed a lot of life into eleven months, not a year, but close.

He was flying Olympic to Chicago, and the return of the same aircraft would take his father to Greece. They would meet at the airport, his father having driven up from Hot Springs, and from there, Paul would return after a day in the Windy City to drop by the university and see old friends, one in particular named Ridje.

After the mandatory hug, his father still held him by the elbows but leaned back to see him more fully. "You are thin, son. Are you well?"

"Yeah, Dad, I'm great. Never been better."

"But you are thin."

"True, but thin is the way to be when I'm a soldier. Remember how hard it was for me to do a single push-up when I was a pudgy teenager the night before I started freshman high school at Oklahoma Military Academy? Now I do push-ups with one hand and pop it off the ground on the way up."

"You dark. I hope you have no trouble in Arkansas. You should stay out of the sun and public for time to fade more white."

"That's already happened, Dad. I told you your friend Jones wouldn't let me in the Paramount Theater just after we got back from Florida that first time."

"I don't remember."

"Yeah, the ticket seller at the entrance wouldn't sell me a ticket. Told me to go to the Negro section of the Malco. I said I wasn't Negro, but Greek, and she said she couldn't see any difference, and I asked to speak to the manager 'cause I knew it was Mr. Jones and he would vouch for me. Well, he looked me over good and said, 'Paul, until you turn white again, I can't let you in.' So, I complained, 'But Mr. Jones, you know me. I'm Paul, John's son.' He answered, 'I know you, Paul, but the other customers don't. I can't let you in.'"

"Things much worse now, Paul; still a lot of unrest. Be careful."

"I will, Dad, don't worry, and when I'm out in the sun, I'll use suntan lotion instead of olive oil."

"How is mother?"

"She's brown too; you'll be surprised. But not only by that. I've never seen her so mellow. You might even enjoy yourself."

"I hope so, Paul. I am tired.

"Couple of months in Greece, Dad, and you'll feel fine."

"Yes, I will.

"You know what you need for hotel. You have busy October. The crowd comes, and many of them this year. A few small conventions, a couple of dinners, but Andy is good. He take care of everything. You just oversee. Money in bank for taxes and three payrolls. You have no problem there. Take better room than 206."

"No, Dad, it's the worst room, and I always stay there."

"You could go to house."

"No, 206 is fine. I leave in the morning and only return to sleep."

* * *

Paul waited with his father for the boarding call, and then he found the Caddie in the bewildering parking lot and drove from O'Hare to Evanston and through the city to the lakeshore and the Northwestern campus. But first, he would go to the Hut, his hangout throughout his four years at the university; if Ridje was in town, she would have left a message for him with Irv and Hank, the Jewish brothers, master pastrami sandwich makers both, proprietors of the coffee house.

Paul had toyed with the idea of writing a book about that time and that place. There would be little action, people coming and going, orders being served, cigarettes lit, millions of cups of coffee drunk. The fellow students he had known there were, like him, outcasts from one point of view, those who avoided the heavy-conformity dependency the fraternity/sorority system imposed on social mixing from another. Of the student body, there were the patrons of the Hut, and the others, like the Greeks, who called all non-Greek speakers barbarians. Hank and Irv saw to that; they refused to serve a potential patron not because of color, race, creed, sex, or orientation, but rather, they would suffer no conservative person, and they judged liberalism on sight, not that a lot of Republican types wanted to frequent their joint anyway. So, the story's real action would be in dialogue covering all the things that were said or implied by all young men and women seeking to find themselves.

"Paul, long time," Hank said.

"How are you, Hank? Yeah, a year and a summer. How's Irv?"

"Irv's well, thanks. Ridje was in an hour ago, looking for you."

"Great!" Paul exclaimed; jet lag be damned, a lover was near. "How can I find her?"

"Sit down and wait. She'll be back."

"And in the meantime, Hank, I've been longing for your pastrami and a cup of joe."

Paul had not considered that after eating a Hank's special returning-friend-and-customer sandwich, he would become drowsy even as he drank three cups of coffee and smoked five cigarettes.

Ridje snuck up on him from behind and goosed him in both sides of his ribs just as she had done the first time they'd met, three years ago.

"Gotcha," she laughed.

Paul levitated a foot off the seat of the barstool he was sitting upon. His heart raced, and he was instantly awake.

"Christ, Ridje, don't stop my heart to say hello."

"Why not?" Ridje asked and then gave her reason: "If you had really missed me, you would have been on the lookout and not half-asleep over your coffee."

"I was for the first hour and a half. After that, Hank's pastrami took over. But you're looking great, Ridje."

"Yes, thank you, I feel good. And it's nice to have you back. Necessary, as a matter of fact."

"You mean I'm not an elective?"

"That too."

"Why necessary, then?"

"I'll tell you later, but now let's move to a booth—one just opened—and get on with relating our experiences."

"What, no kiss? Just talk?"

"Plenty of kisses, but those later too."

After they moved to the booth and had seated themselves side by side, Ridje darted in and gave him a peck on the cheek.

"That's just a quick hi. A full hello depends on your response to my story."

"Okay," Paul replied quizzically.

"First, I live in a rural town in Northern California and teach at the country high school. I won't tell you where because I never want to see you there."

"Thanks a lot."

"No, I don't quite mean it that way. You're an urban not a countryside man. And yes, there is somebody I don't want you to meet. He lacks self-confidence, not much education beyond high school, works at a menial job, and would lose what little nerve he has if he were to meet you, my previous lover to him. Do you see?"

"I'm beginning."

"No, you're not. Josh—that's his name—is really a unique person. He is so gentle wild animals come to him. When we go out into the woods for a picnic, I stop at a certain point, but he goes on another twenty, thirty yards and finds a place—one that he hunts for, mind you—and when he finds the aura he's looking for, he sits and becomes very peaceful, and the wild birds and squirrels and other little beasties—that's what I call them—come near him. Often, birds perch on his shoulders or knees, and squirrels and chipmunks and hares gather close to him. I've even seen a coyote lay down in the undergrowth ten yards away, but the amazing thing is that none of the animals seem to fear any of the others when they are gathered around him. He sits that way for an hour, sometimes more, especially when I am not with him. He never feeds them; that's not the kind of relationship he wants. He seems to have the power of communication with other animals. Nothing intellectual, all feeling and peace. He talks quietly to them, making little gurgling sounds. Then he bows to them, forehead to the ground, and thanks them for their company and the forest for its, and then he'll get up as the animals disperse and come back to me and we have our picnic."

"A Whitman-type poet?"

"Yes, how did you know?

"It figures. So, you love your natural man?"

"I do, but there's a problem."

"Which is?"

"He's the same way as a lover. He's so tender and gentle sometimes I go mad for a wild fuck in our old style, seven pillows under my ass and a jackhammer in my cunt, and I think of you, but I can't spur him on. I tried in the beginning, but it just put him off. So, I have to be more passive than his passivity, and that's not me. But what can I do? I love him, his humanity, his earnestness, his candor, his love of life and all creatures. I mean, he is an ideal human being in most ways.

"And another thing, I don't want someone with my education in the superficial; I want a man who knows the natural world, and that's Josh."

"I can see you in that environment, Ridje. My only concern would be to wonder if it will satisfy you in the future?"

"Paul," Ridje wailed softly, "is there a future? Look at what's happening with Russia over their missiles in Cuba. We could already be at war and are just seconds away from hearing the warning sirens that can only screech the news that the missiles have been launched and are on the way, and there's not a damned thing we can do. I try not to think about it all, Paul, but I can't stop myself. I don't have Josh's tranquility."

"Is he in avoidance?"

"No, he is aware of the dangers."

"How does he react to them, then?"

"As if they belong to a contingent but distant other reality. But it's not avoidance; he doesn't hide from or deny anything. He simple thinks that the future will happen as it happens."

"Well, yeah, that makes sense."

"What I mean is that he thinks the future is determined but only by its happening, and what happens is uncertain, not determined. We may destroy ourselves, we may not, but most likely, we will continue tottering between yes and no, between creation and destruction."

"Obviously, you love an exceptional man. Maybe that should be enough?"

"Should it? Yes. But is it? No. Isn't that the common problem? We all want more. I want a shot of you in Josh. I want the Jack the Ripper ravisher in a saint."

Paul laughed. He put his arm around Ridje's shoulder and pulled her to him, planting a breath in her ear and a kiss on her cheek. "Something I don't understand. Do you have to decide about Josh immediately, or do you have time to see how it develops between you?"

"Rather immediately, unfortunately," Ridje replied. "He has asked me to marry him. He is deeply concerned about the differences in our educational levels, and he worries that, as you said, in time, that may become an insurmountable obstacle between us, so he prefaced asking me to marry him by saying that he wanted me to think carefully—a month, three months, however long I needed —before I answered. I know him, his character; he offers his soul to his wife, to his woman, and wants to receive from her absolute devotion and commitment."

"That sounds consistent with the other things you've said about him, and probably, if he really is the man you describe, he's capable and also worthy of it."

"So?" Ridje said and paused.

Paul sensed what the next subject would be, and he refused to help, "So?" he asked.

"Don't be coy."

"What about you?"

"Answer, will you give me a comparison fuck?"

"You know I'm always on for sex, but what exactly is a comparison fuck?"

"You're still avoiding. You know what I mean."

"Guess what?"

"What?" she asked.

"Yes, because I want to compare you to Judy and I think you'll enjoy the things she's taught me. I'm a much better lover now than I was with you."

"Judy," Ridje responded and sat back. She had not considered the question from Paul's angle. "Who's Judy?"

"The English woman I've been living with in Greece."

"Are you thinking of marrying her?"

"There's the rub, Ridge. You met my mother; she didn't like you."

"I don't think she would care for any woman who was your girlfriend."

"That's all changed, only on the surface, of course. I wrote them that I had found my ideal situation, had an English friend who spoke Greek, and that I was thinking of staying in Greece permanently by enlisting in the Greek army. They went nuts, especially Mother. She came to Greece to save me about seven weeks ago, but on a long trip over by freighter, her friend and traveling companion, Mary, suggested that she use reverse psychology on me, since direct resistance had always failed in the past and was bound to fail in the future. So, when Mother and I met, she was not her usual difficult self. We went to eat, and she talked to me like I was a real person and not just a son. Said that if I loved Judy enough to live with her day by day, and that was the hard part of relationship, that I probably loved her enough to marry her. Blew my mind away. What am I, twenty-three, and she'd never spoken to me like that before. Later, I learned that her suggestion, and probably also her very friendly acceptance of Judy was all part of this reverse psychology business. Well, finding that out sent me into a tail spin until I realized that the reverse could be reversed. Plus, I have the army shit to get through. What they don't know, and I only found this out myself recently, is that if I volunteer for the regular army, which entails a three year tour of duty, I can select where I want to serve or what I want to do. I can't get another deferment, and I'll be drafted in January. So, I'm going to smash the thing head on. I'm going to enlist and select my duty station as U.S. Army Europe, and if I'm really lucky, the army will send me to Greece, and if not, still somewhere in Europe, which is where I want to be. But that doesn't solve the problem of how I'm going to get through three years in the army without a constant woman. I'll be sane and will probably avoid the brig if—excuse the expression—I'm fucked down. But if I report to duty with blue balls, I'll screw up for sure and get a court-martial and do prison time. Yuk!"

"If I've understood your farce, your mother encourages you to marry a woman she doesn't approve of in depth so that you won't marry her, and you now have their permission to do what you don't want to do, but you think that you must do it to keep three years of military service from becoming thirty years of incarceration for involuntary manslaughter, or some such crime."

"You summed it up, Ridje."

"So, what are you going to do?"

"What are you going to do?

"Let's go fuck," they said in unison.

"But don't do it here," Hank said in passing along the aisle.

"We'll drive to the outskirts. There are motels along Highway 30."

"Ha, I'm ahead of you. I have one, but there's a problem," Ridje stated and looked at her wristwatch. "I'm late already."

"For what?"

"Diner with friends, and I must leave now. Look, here's the key. I'll get back as early as I can but before midnight is out. Leave the door unlocked if you take a nap, and I'll wake you with a nice surprise."

They separated; Paul wandered around campus, reminiscing, and then he drove to the motel to sleep for strength when they would perform their comparison ruts. Ridje went to her friends' home, but she never made it back to the motel room because she had such fun that she drank more than she could hold soberly and passed out on their couch. When Paul woke up in the morning, Ridje had not returned. He had no choice, he convinced himself, and he left her a note saying that he had to be in Hot Springs that evening, sorry they'd missed each other. He hoped she was fine. He included his address in finishing and then left the key on the desk, got in his father's car, and headed south, back to Arkansas.

A week later, he received a short letter from Ridje. The envelope bore no return address, and the postmark was San Francisco. "Sorry," the message said, "I got back late morning, but you had already left. I understand. I read your note. Maybe comparisons are not the best idea; probably both of us should just dive in and see where we come out. It's all about learning anyway, isn't it? Be well, Ridje."

* * *

He passed Fountain Lake and laughed remembering that he and his cousin Nicky and just about every other juvenile boy who was straight used to peep through the holes their multitudes had opened in the back panels of the continuous lockers that, along one wall, separated the women's from the men's dressing rooms. Seeing a tit was heaven, spying a snatch was bliss, but they'd been young.

Only a few more miles, and Paul would be back to where he didn't want to be. Passing the intersection of 7 South and Gulpa Gorge Road, the highway turned into Park Ave. Memories cascaded through his thoughts; something had happened everywhere even if it was just a breeze playing a tree leaf.

Just off the avenue, on a side street leading to Ramble School, where he had been a part-year third grader, an old wooden garage door bore a white painted word: "FUCK." When he had asked his mother what the word meant, the storm that had followed had devastated whatever joy new knowledge might have given him. If he'd been sly, he would have muttered loud enough for his mother's keen ears, "Oh, fuck!" Her reaction was predictable.

"What did you say?"

"Nuthin'."

"Yes, you did. I heard you!"

This was the moment that even a clever boy could suffer a slap.

"Just something I heard at school" was the perfect way of transferring blame from himself to the authorities and the other dirty little boys. "Don't mean much, just that somethin' didn't go right."

"That's not what it means. It's dirty!"

If he got through the next second, he was safe. "I didn't know that. Just what I read and heard." As he spoke the word "heard," he had to fill its sound with innocence. like "her-er-erd."

"Well, in the future, stay away from those boys."

"No," Paul interrupted; facts were precise. "We all saw it painted on an old wooden garage door."

"Well, and places like that as well. It's nasty, nasty, don't ever use it again! Do you hear me?"

With a "Yes, Ma" he was free. He had rattled his mother but not paid a price; could it get any better? Whereas, if he stated the facts, which was what he did, he always suffered, "Mother, what does f, u, c, k mean?"

When she put the letters together and was horrified by their meaning, her right hand—or her left; she was ambidextrous—would fly out to slap him across the lips, automatic reaction.

"Where'd you hear that?"

"Ouch! It was painted on a door. I didn't do nothin'."

"You said a nasty word, and I'm going to soap your mouth out."

"But I didn't say it."

"You spelled it, and that's worse."

He was of a size and strength that taxed her limit, and as she started to drag him to the bathroom to wash his mouth out with soap, as she said she would, he broke free from her grasp and was out of the yard and up the street toward the schoolyard before she could command him to come back, as if he would.

On his right-hand side, Paul drove past the Vapors Club Casino and Restaurant. They let him in—even when he had been underage—because they knew his dad, and he only played the slots. Now that he was back, he would go there often. The Velda Rose Motel across the street, the Ramada Inn on this side, and the Majestic and the roundabout onto Central Avenue, and there it was, a block ahead, the DeSoto Hotel, intended to be his one day. And it was beautiful, but in his mind, it was like a gorgeous jailbait chick he'd screwed and gotten pregnant. And then a half a block from the intersection of Central Avenue with Canyon Street, he passed the Black Orchid, his favorite strip joint bar, where his friend C.C. was bartender. At the corner, he turned left across traffic and drove up Canyon Street to the parking lot at the back of the hotel. He switched off the motor, having shifted the transmission into park and applied the foot break. He paused, lit another cigarette, and sat still and relaxed as he informed his person that he was back but not down. He also admitted how foolish he had been: he could have spent another night with Ridje in Chicago; the hotel would have survived four days without a family member present. It had before; it would again. Why had he rushed off? Because his male vanity objected to subjecting himself as an object of comparison. That was stupid. He knew it. He often made mistakes that became clear later, but he wondered why right choices never seemed as defined and in focus as blunders. But upon reflection, he realized that he might never have made a correct decision, but that couldn't have been just by the expectations of probability. He snuffed the butt out in the ashtray, took a deep breath and held it, rolled up the window, stepped out of the Caddie, exhaled, adjusted his expression, and walked into the building; the manager was on duty.

9: CLOSE THE DOOR AND YOU'RE SWEATING AGAIN

Room 206 was as dismal as Paul remembered it being; it was on the inside corner of the long leg of the building's L shape, had two windows on the walls of the outer corner, both looking out on parking decks, and it was directly above the rear maintenance service bay, where the natural-gas-fired heating and air conditioning system was located, but that was useful, as hearing irregularities in the machinery's functioning was part of the room's ambiance and the manager's duties. The toilet was replete with an afterthought micro shower. The closet was built into the wall just beyond the door on the right-hand side and in front of the bathroom. Furnishings consisted of a double bed, a chest of drawers, and a small desk with chair. It had been Jimmy's abode when he'd worked at the DeSoto, and they both preferred it for the same reasons. It was spartan but functional, and its use reduced potential revenue loss less than any other accommodation.

Its only remarkable feature was scraped into the wooden door, panel and frame, where an ardent, middle-aged, widow had clawed at it, begging Jimmy to let her in, but he had resisted. In all other ways, the woman was a good client, and so, the door suffered silently.

The hotel staff welcomed him, and they happily accepted his management, as he was far more courteous than Jane and more forgiving than John, but no pushover, just reasonable.

He had three months to decide on many important issues. His age had reached the branching point in life; on trees, nature imposes a minimum height above ground level for lateral expansion, so must a man have gained at least formative knowledge about the world and its inhabitants in order to chart a course for his own passage within the whole. Paul's mind was raucous; thoughts, especially negative, skated, skipped, slithered, and slunk through his brain, leading nowhere except back to the beginning. The Möbius strip was a trap. He had to get off the Ferris wheel of complaint. Yet as he tried to think in terms of reason, a hot flash of anger or self-pity or both would obliterate his train of thought and jerk him back to the beginning, or end, or never-ending middle of where he had started, no wiser than before, just more used.

Of course, before tackling the serious stuff, he first had to address immediate necessities: a woman and dope. Paul had continued his diet: fresh fruits and vegetables, not as tasty or fresh as in Greece, but better than the alternatives, and no yogurt worth the name; he'd have to make his own. Pieces in place, he could, or would, or should, but must settle himself and plan. As if he had choices. No, yes, he did; he just needed magnification to see them. The army—military service anyway—was there in front of him. There was cogent reason to serve as little time as possible, an equivalent to incarceration, especially now, his early twenties, when he needed to be breaking down the barriers to the future he wanted.

But what did he want? He had seen little in life that was admirable—a lot of it was not even plausible, least of all to himself—so that modeling on a prototype of behavior was impossible.

Something. He knew he wanted something. It was there, out there, not often, rarely if ever mentioned by others, the sense of fulfillment that compensates for the sure knowledge of inevitable death awaiting everyone. Was it an escape from the prison of Edenic asylum and the assumption of the mantle of self-responsibility? Something of that nature, but it also had the dream of a solid personal existence. He had sensed the realness of his father, his uncles, and a few others. He wanted that, to be real.

To be real? Same question, different words.

Would the fog ever lift? Could he be quiet for enough time to exist whole instead of shimmering like a chimera.

Dope was the answer. Hakim had taught him that. He had no contacts, and a source would be harder to find than a woman, so pussy after weed.

On the fourth morning of his continuous shift—in some fashion, he worked from open to shuteye, not a normal day of labor —he noticed two women who were wearing Downtowner Hotel maid uniforms sitting side by side and talking/giggling at DeSoto Restaurant's coffee counter.

From the back, they seemed very similar in figure, and they were wearing the same silly starburst maid's headpiece that distracted from the colors of their hair, both gathered into pony tails, a light brunette and a sandy blonde.

"Hi," Paul said as he walked around behind the counter in the service area. "I've seen you in here the last couple of mornings."

"Wow, isn't he observant?" the blonde taunted.

"You're new. Did you just start working here?" the brunette asked.

"Yeah."

"What's your position?"

"I'm the general fill-in flunky."

"Fill-in?"

"You know, for any employee who can't get to work for some reason. Maid one day, dishwasher the next, and then desk clerk or maintenance man. Just depends on what's needed."

"And you can do all those jobs?"

"Not as well as the employee I replace, but well enough to get by till they return."

"A man for all seasons."

"I think you mean reasons, but if not, then I like spring, but winter is coming."

"And a poet!"

"Blades of grass."

"You like grassy things?"

"Love 'em, but I can't find any."

"No problem, we've got that covered. If you are asking, of course."

"I am and more."

Their faces displayed more age than their figures. Paul judged that they were between thirty and thirty-five.

"Where can we find you at five when we get off?"

"Anywhere you want."

"Parking lot behind, your side; it's more secluded. How about two dime bags?"

"Done," Paul said enthusiastically, and then he introduced himself. "I'm Paul."

"We're Gretel and Gretchen," the brunette said.

"Sisters?"

"Cousins, our mothers were."

They met as planned and then continued walking up the mountainside path. Gretchen had rolled a joint, and she lit up once they were out of anyone's view.

After a few tokes and passing the reefer on, she said accusingly, "You didn't tell us the truth. You're the owner's son."

"But I did. I just didn't give what I thought was unnecessary information."

"You could have bragged to impress us."

"Good God, why would I brag? Reality is hard enough."

They continued on the path that quickly leveled out and wound around behind the sprawling edifice of the Arlington Hotel, the Hot Springs art deco shrine to wealth where Chicago gangsters had permanent suites.

"How old are you, Paul?" Gretel asked.

"Twenty-three. Why? Do I look wet behind the ears?"

"Pathetic. What do you do for sex?"

"Ah," Paul said, stalling, but then he decided. "I just got here—to Hot Springs, I mean—and I haven't had time to address that issue yet."

"What do you think about us?"

"About you?" Paul replied, stalling again.

"Yeah, we're working girls. Oh, we change sheets and fluff pillows, but we are at the Downtowner to service customers' other needs. You should have girls like us at the DeSoto too."

"I know; Dad would be agreeable, but Mother would shoot him first."

"Backed up, is she?"

"Totally."

"But they're not here now."

"Right, gone for three months."

"Then let us work the DeSoto too until they get back, and we'll give you the boyfriend rate."

"All right," Paul enthused, one stop shopping. "But—"

"And there's a butt, if you take my meaning," Gretchen teased.

"No, this is the other kind. But when they get back—before they get back—you've got to stop working in the hotel."

"That's no problem. We're leaving for Nevada at the end of October. Business here is terrible until the end of February."

"Perfect," Paul agreed. "By February, I'll probably be in the brig. But here's another problem. How will you come in with your customers?"

"Give us a key to the back door. We will make the dates out of the hotel; otherwise, you could be implicated. Then the john goes to his room in normal fashion, and we—one or both—meet him there having come into the hotel through the back door. That way, the hotel is not responsible."

"How's that?"

"The client's choice. We pimped him; you didn't."

"I see," Paul replied, impressed by the ladies' command of legal subtleties, completely overlooking another potentially flammable legal question: how had they gotten the back-door key?

"Plus, that way, we don't owe you a portion of our take other than special rates for you."

"Sounds like a good plan," Paul agreed, knowing that his mother would spin in her grave long before she died if she discovered his whoremongering in her hotel. And he considered the arrangement a covert force for reversing reverse psychology.

They had descended from the hikers' path and returned to Central Avenue via Fountain Street, passing the classics of the city's architecture, the Murphy House, the Park Hotel, the Arlington Hotel, the Medical Arts Building, the Opera House that would soon be razed by money hungry idiots to make more parking lots, and they parted in front of the DeSoto. To demonstrate the method, as if it needed to be, Gretel and Gretchen continued across Canyon

Street and re-entered the Downtowner in order to leave it by the rear exit and cross over quickly to the rear of the DeSoto, where Paul would be waiting with the back door that fell at the level of the second floor open for them, and then it was but a step into his dismal room.

"This is your room!" Gretel demanded. "It's a dump."

"It's not that bad," Paul replied defensively.

"It's a dump," she repeated.

"Couldn't you have taken a nicer room?" Gretchen asked.

"Yeah, but why? I'm hardly in it, only to sleep."

"You should see the penthouse our boss has," she added.

"Sorry you don't like it," Paul replied, "and I hope it's not a deal-breaker."

"How's the bed?" Gretel asked, but she pounced upon it to answer her own question. "Not bad," she judged.

"Look, Paul, here's the thing. If Gretchen and I are going to spend any time in this room with you, we will have to feminize it a bit. Make it cheery. You won't mind, will you, dear?"

"No, no, not a bit. Call me when you want to put your touch on it, and I'll let you in."

"Don't be such a prude," Gretchen scolded. "You're giving us a key to the back door of the building. Give us a key to your room as well. We won't filch anything," she added, "and looking around, you don't have anything worth stealing."

Paul was not comfortable with giving the ladies his room key, but since the back-door key by itself was a step into the deep, he might as well plunge deeper.

"Okay," he agreed, and his future dead mother's spin rate went up orders of magnitude. "But," he insisted, and to make his point clearer, he also gestured, waving his hand back and forth with forefinger pointed and the others closed into a thumb-first fist, "no one else, period."

"Oh, Paul, be sensible. We wouldn't bring johns here. If we did, we'd owe you, don't you see."

Even if he didn't see, Paul knew he could not—no, did not want—to reverse the reversal of the reverse.

* * *

After ten days, Paul had found his rhythm. He was fulfilling his necessities and was ready at last to think seriously about his imminent life decision when his mother's first letter arrived. It was postmarked from Mykonos.

Perfunctory information was hurried—Dad was well—and then Jane got to her subject.

> I cannot begin to express my pain and sadness in having to inform you that Judy is acting in a most alarming manner. We are no longer meeting her for dinner, and the last time, she asked to bring a friend along, and we said fine, thinking it would be a girlfriend, but it wasn't. It was a young man, and they seemed awfully, even unseemly, fond of each other. I was shocked. Dad was hurt. We never asked her to dinner after that. Obviously, we couldn't. If we had, we would have been jeopardizing your interest. But we see her often in village center at night, and she is always in the middle of a large group, mostly men, having a good time. She drinks a lot. And we've seen her twice at Paranga nude, completely, and in the mixed company of her friends. All of them are. For a young woman who is serious about a fine young man, she is acting terribly wantonly, etc.

A second letter arrived five days later and related even more details of Judy's licentious behavior. Epitaphs were less friendly. And then another and another, every few days, heralding ever more strident condemnations of Judy's unforgivable demeanor.

Paul, however, had also received letters from Judy in which the blatant acts of lascivious behavior were described as the ordinary comportment of their friends, nothing different from when he had been present.

In either case, the point was elsewhere. Paul had been dallying with Gretel and Gretchen, often with one alone, sometimes the two together, and he took no offense with Judy fulfilling her needs as he was his. Unfortunately, Judy had implied that she was being celibate during his absence. But he had opened his season for reasoning with the conjecture that if the wife doesn't forget the whore she was before becoming the bride, maybe marriage wasn't such a bad idea. Here was Judy, already becoming wifely faithful even before he had proposed marriage.

Finally, in the middle of November, two weeks after Gretel and Gretchen had started plying their trade in Nevada and two weeks before his parents returned, and in the middle of feeling low on both accounts, not having found a replacement for the former and dreading the confrontation promised by the latter, Paul wrote to Judy's father asking her hand in marriage. Of course, he had asked Judy first and was following her request with the father bit. As he mailed that letter, he felt a strong twinge of pain in his left palm; was it the first nail being driven into his flesh for crucifixion?

He had visited the army recruiting office often, become friendly with the sergeant in charge, read the enlistment contract carefully several times, and was satisfied that he would serve his tour in Europe and the extra year added to the two of mandatory service didn't matter, because Europe was where he would have spent it anyway, minus the army. As if more encouragement to enlist rather than be drafted were needed, there was also the difference between eight years of active reserve required from draftees as opposed to six years of inactive reserve duty for enlistees. He also visited the navy recruiter, as everyone accepted the axiom that to become a writer worth one's salt, a young man must first be a sailor, roaming from port to port and story to story. Plus, his father had been a sailor, both military and merchant. But the navy required a minimum four-year tour and made no guarantee of overseas or seaborne deployment. He could easily be stationed at Pensacola Naval Base in Florida, as his cousin Nicky had been.

John and Jane would return on the 30th of November; he could survive two days of parental bombardment, but no more, so Paul signed the papers to enlist in the regular army on Monday, the 3rd of December, 1962. As he signed his name numerous times, the palm of his right hand was pierced by a sharp, quick jab of symbolism; now both his arms were nailed to the cross of the common weal.

There was no choice; the one act made the other necessary. No martyr had ever hung from one hand only, at least, none with whom he was familiar.

The cold war was at fevered pitch, and either Paul had to take the 4-F dodge from the expecting-to-be-kissed back of his father's hand via his influence, or serve in some nation's army, and since he couldn't get back to Greece without a valid passport—and his no longer was—he would enlist in the American, and after the training period, which he had already undergone at military school, he would be sent to Europe, back to his woman, but to live with her freely, he would have to marry her. Thus, he reasoned proposing marriage wasn't his fault; rather, it offered the only sensible means of surviving dull army regimentation.

Life was all quid pro quo, wasn't it? The only question was which did you get the most of, the quid or the quo?

10: LIFE GETS TEEJUS

The backdrop of Paul's three-month stand-in for his parents was the Cuban Missile Crisis. It broke through everyone's attention. Impending doom was in the air; it came down with the rain, sailed in the clouds, filled newspapers and broadcasts. Cabals of Americans held opposing views. Some maintained a range that averaged out at "Better Red than dead!" Others reversed the elements: "Better dead than Red." It wasn't hyperbole; everyone felt the threat, and those who lived in or close to military-grade targets breathed and sweated it. Death was the common factor whether for Red or for red, white, and blue.

Wednesdays at twelve noon was the worst moment of the week: the test of the civil defense siren wailed a condemnation of civilization and culture and intelligence and basic animal dignity, blaring the warning that if it was not exactly noon Wednesday, you were dead but hadn't died yet. (Not to worry, vaporization was instant, so no one would feel a thing—forget the pictures from Hiroshima and Nagasaki.) In a single hearing of the sound, Paul had reached his limit for an epoch, but the shrill insanity of imminent wipe-out was repeated every seven days for a minute.

In a minute, so much could happen. In a minute, the future could become the past, and in a minute, the past could cease altogether. The middle to end of October was a time to live from heartbeat to heartbeat, dreading.

"Would they bomb here?" Gretel had asked.

"Not likely," Paul replied. "We don't have heavy industry or a military base closer than Little Rock."

"But that's only sixty miles."

"More like forty as the crow flies and the wind blows," Paul corrected.

"What about our water? We have three lakes of fresh, drinkable water. If they blew those up, they'd do more damage than anything else in Arkansas, I think."

"Shit," Paul said, "you could be right. I hadn't thought of that, and think about it; if they hit the dam between Ouchitaw and Hamilton, who knows how much water would be lost. What was left of both lakes probably wouldn't fill the bomb crater, and two, if not three, because Lake Catherine would have been knocked away too, hydroelectric generating stations would be down."

"I wonder if that's how they think?" Gretchen asked.

"If we've thought about it, wouldn't they?" Gretel replied.

"They say Cuba is ninety miles off Florida, and that's fifteen hundred miles away from here, maybe we're out of range, I hope."

"Gretchen," Paul said, his voice strangling within him as the thought matured and took form, "if missiles are fired from any-where, they'll be coming from everywhere, over the poles and from under the seas."

"God, Paul, shut up! Shut up! Please. It's so much part of our day. What do you imagine we talk about at work? At least, when we're here with you, can't we just fuck and not think?

* * *

Paul wrote to Judy, telling her that he had received her father's grudging approval of their union and then breaking into silliness:

> . . . on opposite sides of the Atlantic. I don't know how we'll meet, or where. Who will be able to cross? But don't think of coming here. It'll be a mess. Anyway, if we're still alive, we won't want to live here. Two cities I can think of they probably won't bomb are Athens and Paris, because of their special cul-tural value that the victor—whoever it is, if there is one—would miss. Shit, that's stupid. Are they going to give a fuck about cultural monuments? What have you decided? Are you going to London to be with your mother, or are you staying in Greece? Mykonos would be good except for the wind that could blow radioactive fallout right up your nose and down

your throat. I don't know. Maybe this is it. Maybe we'll never meet again. I can't figure anything out, but how can anybody understand what is unimaginable in its true scale?"

Even though he had the working girls' company, they usually screwed him and then left his room, still dismal if brightened, and he had no one to talk to as he had with Judy, and that had become important to him. When potentially general annihilation seemed to be the coming common fate, Paul suddenly realized that he loved Judy. Well, maybe he needed just what she offered, or maybe love was the front line to oppose a looming catastrophe. In his penchant to dive into approaching disaster, he felt proud of himself for proposing marriage before it was moot. The problem would arise if they survived, but that only made sense; the dead don't fret.

Mother is still whining about your behavior. World's falling apart, and she has energy to criticize you for having however much fun you can still have in the time left.

How's Poo?

How's the crew? Jason still broken up? Have Cleopatra and Nick returned?

I'm not making any sense, am I? I can't figure out how I feel. I'm just angry and can't do anything with it. I can't bang our rulers heads together and demand that if they are going to lead their nations, the had no mandate to lead them to oblivion. But it's so obvious. How can anyone not see that everyone wants things their way and if I were in your shoes, I'd want what you want even if it was opposite of what I want in my shoes. Shoes, what, more nonsense. But I can't think. I start, and then my mind is rushed by the palpable tension in the air. What are you doing to hole up?

Paul's letter rambled on. He repeated himself. Didn't matter. As long as he could write, he didn't have to think, because those thoughts had already happened.

* * *

If anyone wanted to witness a miracle, there was no longer need to travel to Lourdes or elsewhere; the sacred event was that human sense prevailed and the species did not begin destroying itself seventeen years after Hiroshima. No one except those who were there —and not all of them—and everyone with his/her own opinion, knows, knew, or will ever know how close nuclear war came to Earth, like a dinosaur-exterminating asteroid that barely missed, just grazing the atmosphere, in the second half of October 1962. In the last moments before mankind's worldwide folly commenced, some ad hoc committees of leaders and advisers realized that they could be Red, and we didn't have to be either Red or dead.

All the lies that for a few moments, evaporated between those negotiating the fate of the world and all its creatures were soon falling again like sludge in the minds of men who would rule other men when they could not, would not, and cannot control themselves.

Paul had to look no further than himself, evaluate his internal ignorance and confusion, and then multiply that miasma many times to feel the weight of leaders' responsibility that was surely beyond the strength of any one or many to fulfill.

At the beginning of November, tensions lessened; Russians and Americans agreed to withdraw nuclear-armed missiles from positions close to each nation's borders. People even began planning for Thanksgiving. Needless to say, Halloween had been a hoot, with many children dressed as X-ray-exposed skeletons. Gretel, Gretchen, and Paul emerged from feeling they were hiding from something even more dismal than his hole in Room 206. Not by changing any action, but simply by change of mind, they would die—hopefully far in the future—from other causes than vaporization or radiation.

Paul received a postcard from his father hoping he was well and asking how the crisis had affected business.

His mother called. Jane was frantic. "I tried to change our tickets to come back immediately. If the war started and we were still in Greece . . . We were lucky to have a booked flight. Forget changing dates; everybody wants to get out. Where is everybody going?" she asked. "Is one place better than the next? Is here better than there? But everything meaningful to us is there. Our lives are there, but we're stuck here. Judy is acting worse than ever. I think she's out of control. Paul, you must be careful, etc."

Unbelievably, life returned to normal—at least, people started lifting their gaze from the pavement or pulling it down from the sky, both futile glances. Judy stayed in Greece. John and Jane returned to their beloved hotel and mortal son. Paul enlisted, did his training, shipped overseas, and cohabited with Judy in Frankfurt, Germany, where he had been stationed.

Judy and Paul completed the numerous steps required by the military to approve a marriage to a foreign national in a four-power-divided and occupied defeated German nation. When the date was set, Paul wrote to his parents and invited them to the wedding in London.

Jane could not forgive her folly. Why had she listened to Mary's advice? She should have continued as she had acted in the past by protecting Paul from himself. His mind wasn't clever enough for reverse psychology to work. He had taken her at her word. She, herself, had encouraged him to marry that British bitch. She already felt as if she had opened the door and pushed Paul out of the car when he was a child. How could she have done it again?

She was restless. Jane needed distraction. Attending the wedding was beyond her understanding. She wouldn't be able to control herself. To witness her son, her only child, ruin his life and her dreams was unbearable.

She was insufferable.

John, to save himself and calm her, suggested that they take a trip to Yellowstone National Park during the same time period as Paul's wedding. Jane accepted. It was too painful for her to remain at the seat of empire, at the beautiful DeSoto Hotel and Baths that would probably not now, or ever, ring with the cheery voices of completely Greek grandchildren, as the dumb bunny crown prince was being castrated in a distant land.

The morning was beautiful—at least, John thought it was—the air crisp in the first signs of the coming fall season. They were on a road in the northern part of the park, traveling from Mammoth

Hot Springs, where they had spent the night in a hotel with the same name.

Jane maintained a controlled frenzy of dread, despair, and disgust. Paul was already married. He had written that the civil procedure would occur at nine o'clock GMT; New York was five hours behind, minus another two for Wyoming, and it was now 10:30 in Jane's dreadful morning, plus two for noon, plus five for 5:30 pm in London. They would be on the train returning to Frankfurt. The deed was done unless God had answered her fervent prayers but hadn't informed her yet.

"Jane," John said, beginning again, as he had so many futile times before, to reason with her, "we must accept fact and make it the best we can."

"You dare say that? Look at you! You've started smoking again. And it's all Mary's fault. You started again around her. One cigarette, and then two. Then it was back to how it used to be. And it's her fault Paul is married."

"You didn't have to follow her advice," John observed as he punched in the dashboard lighter, having decided to smoke in the car—window down, but it would still annoy her.

She wasn't the only one to suffer. Paul wasn't only her son, although that would be hard to tell most of the time. Had she forgotten that Paul had been conceived like any normal child, not with a miraculous event as she sometimes acted. Paul was his son too. John also hurt, but this grinding away at every minute-by-minute detail of what had probably happened and what had been said and what impression had been left and how each understood the other and a thousand other things was too much.

It's over. It's done. Accept it! he thought.

"It's over. It's done. Accept it," he said, and then he inhaled deeply on the cigarette. At least the tobacco smoke was some comfort.

"Look," he said, hoping to distract Jane, if only for a moment, "there are bison over there," and he pointed.

"You say it's over and done. Not for me. I will never accept it, never!"

That was his limit. John slowed the car and pulled it off onto a parking space by a scattering of outdoor tables.

"Jane," he said, and it almost sounded like Ioanna, "if you don't accept Paul's wife, you will drive him away forever, and I won't have it," he finished in a command. "You failed. You told him to do what you didn't want him to do, and he did it. No psychology is meant to be reversed. It was bad advice. Shame on Mary for giving. Shame on you for taking."

She did not respond. That was unusual. He looked at her. Her eyes were wide. She seemed to be trying to say something. He turned to look out the driver's side window to see what she was gawking at through the rear door window on his side and saw the bear.

It had come up on the car from behind. It made noises, and now he could smell it. Its nose was twitching in the partially open window frame, and its runny mucus was dripping on his pant leg.

"Go away, bear," he said and blew smoke in its mitt.

That was John's folly.

The bear blistered from inquisitive to aggressive and jerked its head back as it swatted at the glass. Before John could react, the bear reared up on its hind legs and thumped the top of the car with its front paws. The car rocked. The bear pushed again. The car jostled more. The bear threw its weight against the door, and the car bobbled like a boat in rough seas. John came out of his shock, threw the cigarette toward the bear's head, turned the ignition switch, jerked the gear lever into drive, and floored the accelerator.

They drove in silence after leaving the aggrieved bear in a rush, both of them were staring out the front window.

"You see what having to put up with cigarette smoke is like? I feel like that animal, but I'm civilized."

John pressed the button to lower the window again, but this time he threw out his pack of cigarettes. He would never smoke again.

"Thank you," Jane said.

Those were words he had not often heard from her—and, actually, only slightly more often from Paul.

The fright from the bear had burst through her long-lived cloud of panic and grounded Jane in a useful reality again. John was right. She had to accept Judy. She would. Suddenly she tired of her rant against fact. What was done was done. Judy was her daughter-in-law, like it or not. There was always divorce, heaven forbid.

Actually, if not in reference to Paul, she liked Judy.

After so many years of steadfastly ignoring—not all, but almost all—of her advise, Paul's folly had been to accept Jane's reverse psychology suggestion and marry Judy when his mother did not mean or want what she had advised.

The world, at least, had escaped the folly of war.

Printed in Great Britain
by Amazon

41626696R00089